My CYBORG Savior

Honoria Ravena

Crimson Romance
New York   London   Toronto   Sydney   New Delhi

CRIMSON
ROMANCE

Crimson Romance
An Imprint of Simon & Schuster, Inc.
1230 Avenue of the Americas
New York, NY 10020

For information about special discounts for bulk purchases, please contact Simon & Schuster Special Sales at 1-866-506-1949 or business@simonandschuster.com.

The Simon & Schuster Speakers Bureau can bring authors to your live event. For more information or to book an event contact the Simon & Schuster Speakers Bureau at 1-866-248-3049 or visit our website at www.simonspeakers.com.

ISBN: 978-1-4405-6984-5
ISBN: 978-1-4405-6985-2 (ebook)

For Lindsey, who has always supported me.
The gas station guy still asks me about my "sister."

Acknowledgments

Thank you so much to Debra, you're always there to help me out. Thanks to Megan for being a great friend and beta reader. A special thanks to Jess and everyone at Crimson Romance. I'm so pleased to be working with you all. And lastly a thank you to Candace Havens. Without Fast Draft this would have taken a lot longer to write.

Chapter One

"Jamila."

Jamila turned over and brought one of her pillows along to cover her ears. The intercom was stuck on one volume: loud. It also caught some kind of awful static from the latest and greatest SkyTemple stabilizers. But the stabilizers were necessary. The planet Larus was prone to terrible windstorms that brought a house crashing to the earth at least once a year.

"Jamila," her father's voice carried through the intercom again, "if I send a servant to check on you, and you're asleep, I'll take your shopping allowance away for a week."

That wasn't a big threat, considering she had enough allowance saved to last her a year. And that was if she shopped at the finest tailors in New Kent. If she chose to wear peasant clothing she couldn't begin to guess how long it would last.

Jamila sighed and released her pillow. She hated it when her father was home. He was one of those early risers, while she usually slept till noon. But then, she'd kept one of the servants up till five in the morning flying virtual combat missions over Dramam. Her father would never play games or associate with the "lower" classes.

"Jamila Christianna Clearborne!"

She flinched at the high-pitched squeal of faulty electronics as her father concluded the call. One day she was going to shoot the 'com.

The floor was ice-cold when she rolled out of bed. Another thing that was malfunctioning because of the constant remodels.

When father was home, he seemed to think the place needed fixing.

Jamila slipped her feet into her self-heating slippers and pulled on a silk robe before going to see what her father wanted. She took her time, just to be a pain in the ass. It was an awful day out. In the summer the open, villa type architecture was beautiful. The SkyTemple could be closer to the ocean, so the warm sea breeze could waft through the windows. Now the Temple was higher in the air to avoid waves, and closed up tighter than a tomb. Rain lashed the windows and lightning lit the dark sky.

She tried to shake her case of the bored-as-hell blues. Six more months of this. Luckily, her father was due back at the Senate next week, so she would be able to leave the villa again. He always insisted that it was dangerous outside these walls, and when he was home he had the ability to make her stay…for the most part.

She stifled a yawn with the back of her hand and stretched as she entered the large dining room. She came to an abrupt halt. Father sat on one end of the table and a strange little man with pinched, rat like features sat on the other. To the left, against the wall, a line of dirty, haggard slaves stretched down the length of the table.

One man stood out. He was the tallest, most muscular man she'd ever seen. She was used to being around noblemen, who were usually varying degrees of short and shorter, and tended to be quite thin and frail from the pollution of the cities. At six feet, Jamila was a grotesquely tall woman among the rich, towering over them all. But this man had her by almost a foot.

His hard forearms flexed beneath the thick slave bands he wore. He had dense sleeves of tattoos down his arms. Nobles had given up tattoos long ago as a perverse, disgusting form of body modification. She usually felt the same way about them, but on him, they were extraordinary. Detailed tropical forest scenes with vibrant colors and animals she'd never seen. He only wore loose pants, showing off his chest and tattoos.

When she could close her gaping mouth, she asked, "Father, what's going on here?" She kept her voice as neutral as possible. Disagreeing with her father was never a good idea. If he knew how much she abhorred slavery, he would probably surround her with slaves.

"You need a bodyguard. Someone to protect you and keep you in the house while I'm away."

She swallowed, and tried to think of a good way to wiggle out of this little disaster. "But Father, what could possibly encourage a slave, a criminal most likely, to defend his captor?"

The weasel man spoke. His voice was high pitched and squeaky. "Simple. If you die, they die."

She raised a scornful eyebrow. "For some, slavery is a worse fate than death. I've met many slaves who would die to escape their torment." She turned to her father. "Daddy, I don't think this is a good idea. It could get me killed."

Jamila resisted the urge to roll her eyes. She doubted she was in enough danger to need a bodyguard. This was probably a ploy to get a spy on the senator's side. He didn't want her going out and partying. Last year he couldn't have cared less but this was election year, and he was more paranoid than ever about their image.

He shook his head, his stubborn chin set. "If you die, it would be a fate worse than death for them. The poison that would be released into their system would eat at their insides for over a month before it finally killed them. There is no cure. It's a very slow, agonizing way to go. But if they accept, and keep you alive, they get a warm, soft bed, as much food as they can eat, baths, new clothes, and any entertainment they escort you to. All they have to do is follow a child around. It's not a bad deal."

She tensed. Jamila hated being called a child. It was a sure sign her father was trying to put her in her place and force his will on her. She was twenty-four and far past the need for a babysitter.

It was clear that some of these men were dying for a chance to be a high class servant. Some of the slaves were salivating. Not that she could blame them. They were thin and frail. A few even had bloated bellies—a sure sign of malnutrition. Couldn't this slaver spare one nutrition bar a day to keep them from appearing like they could drop dead at any second? And they were definitely beaten often.

"Well, daughter? Examine them. Choose."

She rolled her eyes. "Most hardly look fit enough for any work, let alone being a bodyguard."

In fact, there was only one that was fit for that kind of duty. Glancing at his ridged body and the angry set of his jaw, she seriously doubted he'd be grateful if she chose him. However, it was her one chance to save him from some other horrible person. Other nobles would take one look at his handsome, stubborn face and have him beaten.

She walked down the line, pretending to consider them. The men didn't get better upon closer inspection. They were even more malnourished than she'd suspected. Some could barely stay on their feet, swaying back and forth, their eyes glazed over. Others smelled awful, as if they couldn't hold their bowel movements.

She stepped in front of the large man, who was chained in the middle of the line. "Tell me about this one? Judging by the others, you must not have had him very long. He's still fit and not diseased." She glanced at her father. "Unless you want to spend an incredible amount of money fixing one of these poor creatures, it would have to be this man."

Her father arched a brow at the slaver, who immediately started his sales pitch. "I don't know about that one. I brought him at your request, but he's a recently captured cyborg. Could be trouble. However, he's been docile. He's perfect for a bodyguard. A martial arts expert. Intelligent. Obedient."

The prisoner's head shot up to glower at the trader, and his electric blue irises seemed to glow. Jamila rolled her eyes. That was the scowl of one obedient criminal to be sure.

"He won't be any trouble if he hopes to live. He's lucky he wasn't executed for abandoning his post."

The man's gaze shot to hers and she jumped. No slave should dare to meet his mistress's eyes. It would get him beaten or executed. Her reaction caught her father's attention.

"What are you doing? Don't you dare meet my daughter's eyes."

The glare he gave Jamila's father was enough to send a shiver down her spine. It was the expression of a killer. A dangerous man. The slaver stomped down his line of pitiful souls and shoved his electric guard stick in the slave's belly. He grunted and doubled over but didn't go down. She gaped at him. Those things had enough voltage to knock a man unconscious and he barely moved. She shivered. Cyborgs were powerful. It wasn't a good idea to keep one as a slave. Especially one that had escaped before.

They were genetically engineered to be faster and smarter than humans and were immune to almost any illness. But unlike normal genetically engineered people, most of a cyborg's joints and bones were reinforced with metal and they were supposed to have some sort of computer enhancing their brains that could put even gen engineered intelligence to shame. Their nanobots helped to speed healing even further. None of that should have increased his ability to resist pain. In fact he was probably more sensitive to everything. What was done to them to make them so resilient?

It wasn't a question she could voice in this room. Her father was against genetic engineering and body enhancements. She couldn't believe he'd considered this man to guard her. Though, he was a slave, and her father probably figured that was a cyborg's rightful place if they had to exist.

"Well, Father, this has to be the one. He's the only one fit for any kind of work."

Her father snorted. "A bit of a stubborn creature. You'll have to tell me if he exhibits any willfulness. He'll have to be punished for it."

Jamila nodded, but couldn't manage to say anything. If she opened her mouth she'd probably tell him he was a bastard for wanting to beat a man who had every right to be "willful."

"How much?" He and the slaver started haggling over the price. Her father was a cheap man, and a hard bargainer. He'd likely get the slave for less than he was worth.

She examined her new acquisition while they bickered. He gave off dangerous vibes that set the hair on the back of her neck on end. No one would mess with this man without facing death. He shifted his stance and rolled his shoulders, displaying fine muscles in his chest. He definitely wasn't what she was used to. There wasn't a feminine feature on his face. His angular jaw was clenched as he stared arrogantly forward, instead of looking down at the ground as he was supposed to. Though, that rule probably wouldn't apply to him. A bodyguard couldn't stare at his feet all day.

Jamila's gaze fell to his tattooed arms and she couldn't resist touching the colorful flesh. Would it feel different than normal skin? She'd never seen anyone with tattoos up close. They were beautiful. She ran her hand along his warm forearm, examining them, and he tensed. When her gaze moved back to his face he was staring down at her and flashed her a crooked smile that made her stomach flip. She removed her hand and stepped away.

"If you don't gain some manners, my father is going to have you beaten. I can't stop him," she whispered.

His gaze slid down her body, male appreciation showing on his face as he scanned her from head to toe. She rolled her eyes. He was sure to get hit often. Would he try to hurt her? It wouldn't surprise her. The man was a criminal, arrogant, and impossibly stubborn. He would probably think her father would free him if he could gain an advantage over him. Such as holding his daughter hostage. Did the slave know what his bands could do if he vexed her father? They could cause more agony than any whipping.

"I'm not afraid of a little pain. It's worth it to watch such a fine woman." His gaze rested on her nipples, hard from the cold. She had the absurd impulse to cross her arms over her breasts. The gods only knew why. The sheerness of her robe was indecent to annoy her father, but plenty of men had seen her topless. Her breasts were probably the most famous ones in the galaxy. That's what happened when you became a drunken party girl who flashed nosy paparazzi while stumbling out of a courtroom. She suppressed a flinch at the memory. She lived to rebel, but the year after her mother's suicide had been a horrible one. She didn't remember most of it.

Jamila shouldn't have been surprised that he spoke to her. He wasn't a normal slave, and clearly hadn't been in the trade long enough to know any better. Most didn't speak at all unless they were asked a direct question. She'd been in some households where slaves' tongues were removed if they broke the rule. She shuddered. She'd have to teach him some hard and fast rules or he was going to end up dead.

Maybe her father would let her free him some day. As soon as the notion came she dismissed it. It wasn't done, and even if she did, as a cyborg he'd go right to one of the Haven districts where the genetically engineered and enhanced people were forced to live. If he wasn't detained or executed by the government. He'd probably have a better life with her.

"Father, if we're done, I'd like to take this man to bathe." Her gaze slid to the slave. "Sorry, but you stink, I'm sure due to these others and the terrible conditions you're likely kept in."

The slave nodded. She was sure he could smell himself, and the people around him. Cyborgs were supposed to have a heightened sense of smell.

Jamila's father flashed a tight lipped smile. "Not yet, daughter. We haven't settled on a price, and I must speak to your slave alone before he begins his duties. He needs specific instructions and some knowledge of how this household is run. I can't have him being as blatantly offensive as he's been so far. Then I will call a servant to take him to you. You're dismissed."

Great, she could go back to bed.

• • •

After what seemed like hours of haggling, the senator had finally settled his price with the slave owner. Galen stood there the whole time, attempting not to yawn and roll his eyes. Why had he agreed to do this? Of all the missions, on all the planets in the galaxy, this was what he'd picked. But he was one of the best at subterfuge, so it made sense. The job hadn't even begun and he already regretted taking it. Though the senator's sexy daughter would probably make it more fun. There was something about her. Galen couldn't quite explain it.

She was sad. And clearly fed up with her father. Not that Galen could blame her. The man was a blowhard. The classic politician. But why was she depressed? No immediate answer came to mind. What could possibly be wrong in the spoiled, little, purebred girl's happy life?

The slaver pulled a remote from his back pocket and hit the release on the chains that bound Galen to the others. There was a crash as they hit the floor and Galen stepped out of the line. None of the slaves tried to flee. They stared at the ground, silent and subdued. Had all the fight been beaten out of these people? He hadn't been among them long enough to know. The trader had been instructed to sell him as soon as possible. That he was dangerous.

Not that the creep was going to mention that to the senator. Even authorized cyborg dealers were greedy little fucks. One day it would be his downfall. If he sold a slave he claimed was perfectly well behaved and it happened to kill someone, the trader would likely go to trial and be executed. But it didn't seem to matter to him as long as he made plenty of money to feed his expanding waistline.

The senator didn't even spare him a glance as he pressed his thumb to the credit scanner. "Sit down, cyborg."

It was on the tip of Galen's tongue to tell him where he could shove his uppity attitude. Thankfully, he'd learned that thinking before you spoke was a better idea. So he sat.

The slaver and his remaining product filed out of the room. "Odious toad," the senator murmured under his breath.

Galen arched an eyebrow. Maybe Cyrus Clearborne did have some good qualities. Or at least knew what made a person a son of a bitch.

He finally looked up. "What is your name?"

"Galen." He didn't add anything more. Most low born people no longer had last names. Identification was so instantaneous that the government felt it was a waste. They were all numbers to them.

"Well, Galen, if you fail me I'll turn you over to the government. As long as you keep my daughter safe, we'll have no problems. She means the world to me, and has no idea how much danger she is in. Most threats to her are idle, but we have had some that have become very specific. They are including details of places she's been. Pictures of her coming and going from shops. There has even been one attempt on her life that was thwarted by my own guards. She knows nothing about it, and you're not allowed to tell her. While my staff investigates this new threat, you'll be responsible for making sure she's safe at all times. That girl better not even get a splinter while under your care, or we'll have to re-evaluate your place in life."

Galen nodded. He knew how it was going to be. It was what he'd been sent for. But he doubted the man's love for his daughter. He had no caring note in his voice when he spoke about her. The majority of the new threats his daughter was getting were from Galen's own people, but word of these pictures of her worried him. His people hadn't been sending those.

"I also have additional tasks for you. My only child has a bit of a rebellious streak."

That was putting it lightly. There probably wasn't a thing that girl hadn't done, and the whole galaxy had probably seen her do it.

"I'd like you to keep her out of embarrassing situations. No partying, no flashing the cameras, no drug use or drinking, no getting arrested, and no sex. The voters already think she's a whore, and I think she spends way too much time in bed with too many different men. I'm going to marry her off, and I'd like for some of the horrible rumors to fade before the wedding, so the groom isn't bombarded with stories about the men she's been 'dating.' Elections are next year. I need this girl's reputation to become, and stay, sparkling clean until then."

Galen hadn't expected that. How was he supposed to keep a well-known party girl from doing what she wanted? Especially since she could threaten to have him killed if he didn't do what she said.

"Now, I know she's likely to threaten you, but you'll have to hold your ground. As long as she doesn't come to me with allegations of rape, I'll assume you're doing what I've asked, and give you the benefit of the doubt."

"And if she comes to you with allegations of rape? Which she'll probably do as soon as she figures out it's the only thing that will get me off her back."

A harsh edge entered the man's voice. The first sign of emotion Galen had seen. "I'll have her examined. If you have raped her, you'll be castrated and handed to the government."

Ouch. *Don't fuck boss's daughter* was going straight to the top of his no-no list. That was a damned shame. She was a fine piece. Probably wouldn't touch him anyway. Well-bred women were like that. They seemed to think that genetic engineering and cybernetic systems could be passed like some disease, when in reality, a team of doctors had to be very determined to turn you into what Galen was. He didn't want to lose his cock for some slutty senator's daughter anyway. He'd already have one scar from this mission, he didn't need any more. The barcode burned into his flesh might come out with cosmetic surgery, but there was no way to be sure.

"Do you understand, slave?"

"Of course."

Cyrus raked a hand through his graying hair before crossing his arms over his chest. He was in remarkable shape for his age and station in life. Most nobles were thin and frail. There were few that were healthy enough to gain weight, but Cyrus maintained his appearance. Why? "I want you to comprehend how much danger she's in. My political rivals aren't above having us both killed."

"Then why don't you have a bodyguard?"

"I have several assigned to me, like the rest of the senate. And she's no doubt safe while I'm here. But I'm leaving soon. Not only does she have my political rivals to deal with but she's also generally disliked by everyone." The senator nodded. "Now if you'll go with Louisa, you can bathe, and attend to my daughter at once."

Chapter Two

Jamila wasn't able to go back to sleep after her encounter with the slave. Was her father threatening him now, or giving him instructions? The door to her rooms slid open and a line of servants filed in. She pushed herself up.

"What are you doing in here?"

They marched to her closet, gathered a row of clothing, and left the room without answering her. "Hello? What are you doing?"

The slave appeared at the entrance. "Get up, and get dressed. You're moving. I'm Galen, by the way, so you don't have to continue to call me 'slave' as I'm sure your father will."

"What?" Outraged, she jumped off the bed. He couldn't just move her wherever he pleased. Her foot got tangled in the thick blankets and she would have tumbled to the ground if he hadn't grabbed her.

"I can't guard you here. I need to be close. We need adjoining rooms."

She shook her head and pushed away from him. "That's unacceptable. I enjoy my privacy, Galen. I won't be sharing a room with you." She couldn't bear to have him that close. He was beautiful, and virile, and so much more attractive than any male she'd been near. But after her recent escapades she was taking a man break.

He arched an eyebrow. "I didn't say sharing a room, I said adjoining rooms. And you don't have a choice. It's my job to protect you, and considering what will happen to me if I fail, I'm not going to take no for an answer."

She shook her foot to untangle it and stumbled away from him as she broke free. "Well, I'll go to my father about this. It's inappropriate for us to share a room. He'll object."

He flashed her a tight lipped smile. "You'd be wrong. I cleared it with him. Don't worry, princess, you'll be settled in another room by the end of the day, and you won't even have to do any of the work to get there."

Jamila rolled her eyes. "That's not the point. I like this room." She didn't really care. All of the rooms were the same. There was no reason to object to moving, except that she didn't want to share a room with this man. She wouldn't be able to get away from him if he lived right next to her.

She opened her mouth to argue with him, and paused. Maybe she should see this as an opportunity. Her father had only bought him to keep her safe. What if she could get him to admit to her father that he couldn't manage it? She'd chased off plenty of others. Tutors, men, governesses.

She glanced at Galen. None seemed as formidable as he did though, and it was already proven that he was stubborn. Also, she had to consider if she could do it without getting him killed. She didn't want that, no matter how pushy and unwanted he was in her life. Still, she could annoy the hell out of him, and maybe he'd crack. Then she could ask her father to release him.

His eyes narrowed, as if he could see what was going on in her head. She smiled, trying to appear every inch the sweet Daddy's Girl. It took all her will not to roll her eyes. She wasn't good at playing the innocent sweetheart.

"Actually, I think that would be a good idea. I could use a servant always at my beck and call."

He crossed his arms over his wide chest. "I'm not a servant. I won't do anything but be your bodyguard."

She smirked. "Now, I'm sure my father would object to that. You're a slave, after all. You're supposed to do what I say. I'm sure you were told what orders you should ignore, but I bet my father didn't say I couldn't order you around."

She flinched internally. She hated to be a bitch to the man, but the sooner she could get rid of him, the better. If she had to be horribly spoiled she would.

"Now, if you'll help the servants move the bed, I'd like to get back in it. I was up late."

"No, you're done sleeping. You were awake when we walked in."

How dare he? He was going to order her around now? Of all the pompous, arrogant men she'd ever met, he was quickly becoming the worst.

"I'll sleep when I please, and if I want to lounge around and spend my days in bed you can't stop me."

He bent over and tossed her over his shoulder, provoking more of her ire. Jamila squeaked and pounded his back with her fists. She tried to straighten, so he'd be forced to let her go, but he shifted her so she couldn't hold her own weight. She collapsed against his hard back, cursing him.

"You, find her something to wear, and get her into it." He strode toward her bathroom, set her on her feet, and pushed her inside. "Shower, do whatever other girly thing you have to do. Hair, makeup, what have you, and get dressed. Don't make me come in there after you. You won't like it if I have to dress you."

She rolled her eyes but the heat in his voice made her insides quiver. Somehow she doubted she'd dislike it if he dressed her. Though she'd rather have him undress her. His dominance sent a little shiver down her spine. She should have found it repugnant, but it was thrilling. No nobleman would have treated her like that. And she would have fed him her fist if he dared.

She shook her head and turned on the shower. She glanced over her shoulder and found him watching her, his appreciative gaze on her backside. She straightened, stomped to the door, and slammed it in his face. "When someone has my clothes, you can open that again. Why don't you do something useful instead of watching my ass?" she shouted.

"But, princess, it's my job to watch your ass."

She kicked the door with her bare foot and then cursed as pain shot up her leg. She could hear his deep, robust chuckle through the closed barrier. Damn that man. Five seconds into his company and she already wanted him gone. At least the fact that he was being pushy would help her feel less guilty.

She threw off her robe, stepped into the shower, and started her morning routine. Or, rather, her afternoon routine. She was rarely up this early. It was only nine. She yawned and stretched as the warm water rushed over her body.

How dare her father do this to her? Despite the many death threats made, her father had never bothered to assign her a bodyguard. And no one ever acted on threats against her, even though she was out often among noblemen and peasants alike. But many people tried to murder her father. He was trying to trap her, like he had her mother. Panic clawed at her insides.

Was she becoming her mother? Before she'd committed suicide, she'd stayed in bed constantly; she drank and took pills prescribed by the family doctor. Jamila dismissed the idea. She stayed up late, she deserved to sleep in, even if she could barely sleep at all anymore. And her mother drank on the quiet; she didn't party with her friends. By the end of her life she'd barely had any friends left. She'd stopped going out with them.

The whole door shook under the force of the knock from the other side and she jumped.

"What's taking so long, princess?"

She rolled her eyes. It hadn't even been twenty minutes. She had gotten sucked into her thoughts, but it hadn't been that long. "I'll be out when I'm out. I'm not done yet."

"I'm just saying, for someone who probably bathed yesterday, you're taking an awful long time. You can't possibly be that dirty."

Jamila glared at the door but shut off the water and stepped out of the shower stall. He had a point. A normal shower usually took ten minutes. The chemical spray got you clean instantly, and in richer households like this one, a conditioning agent appropriate for hair and body followed. The water ran blue until you were clean. She'd been standing in clear, fresh water for about ten minutes. The de-humidifier kicked on along with the drier, evaporating the water while it dried her hair and body.

She opened the door and poked her head out. "Now can one of the servants hand me clothes?"

He smirked and pulled them out from behind his back.

Jamila snatched them from his hands and shut the door to get dressed. When she stepped out of the bathroom most of the contents of her room were gone. The only thing that remained was the furniture, which was the same in every room, so she didn't need it.

She put her hands on her hips. "Now what?"

"Do you have any plans for the day?"

"Not until this afternoon. So what am I supposed to do until then?"

He shrugged. "It's your house. Surely you have something you can do."

Doubtful. She could go shopping, that was about it. All the servants in the house were busy, so there would be no bomber simulations over some alien planet. If she watched the news, she'd likely be inundated with reports of her father, and herself. In the winter there wasn't much to do. She was in for a boring day.

• • •

Jamila spent the day reading with her ever present guard examining her. Always sitting there like some black cloud. But now it was five in the afternoon. It was a whole different playing field. As soon as the sun set on Larus, the nightlife in the Forbidden District of the city started. Her father had warned her to stay away from there, but she wasn't about to listen. She had a special errand to run before a night of partying kicked off. Now if she could get rid of her black cloud. She was sure he would never approve an outing, particularly one not only into the Forbidden District, but Haven as well which she couldn't allow him to know about.

Galen was currently lounging on his bed in the room next to hers. The door was open so he could keep an eye on her from his reclined position on the bed. She stood and walked over to the door. His eyes were closed, and he appeared completely relaxed. Was the idiot sleeping? It seemed too good to be true. She quietly started to shut the door when he spoke.

"What are you doing, Jamila?"

"So you're not asleep. Great bodyguard you are, lying around with your eyes closed."

"I'm probably more aware of everything asleep than you would be on your best day awake. And since I wasn't sleeping I don't see why you care. Believe me, if someone had come in here, I would have intercepted them long before they could reach you. So I'll ask again: what are you doing?"

Annoyance shot through her. And she'd assumed this would be easy. "I need to dress for dinner. I don't plan on giving you a show."

He opened one eye and peered at her, seeming to accuse her with his gaze. After all, she'd given everyone else a show. "I'll keep my eyes closed while you change."

She snorted. "As if I'd trust you."

Both eyes sprang open. "Princess, you're not my type. And I have a job to do. You don't have to worry about me spying. My concern is that these walls are almost completely soundproof. Even for me, and I have excellent hearing."

She didn't doubt it. Cyborgs had excellent everything. She dragged her gaze down his body. She hadn't quite believed that until now, but staring at him, he was definitely fine everywhere. She shook her head.

"But you can still hear?"

"Yes, but—"

She cut him off by closing the door. She smirked. Mission accomplished. She made quick work hacking the locking mechanism as she'd done in the past. It wouldn't keep him out, that was for sure—he had enough strength to tear a hole in the wall—but it might buy her a few extra seconds.

She'd actually changed in the bathroom a few minutes ago, and she'd opened her window to the bitterly cold wind in preparation for this moment. She wouldn't make a sound as she shrugged out of her robe and slipped out the window and into the fake grass. One good thing about him moving her to this room was that it was on the first floor. She didn't have to do any climbing to escape.

The doorknob rattled as she straddled the ledge of the window.

He banged on the door with his ham handed fist as she slipped out and dashed for the shuttle bay. His move had also put her closer to it than before. She wished she'd thought of switching rooms earlier. She had her pick of the entire Temple. Especially when her father was gone. She'd moved rooms five times in two years, and had never considered that one. She'd been a fool.

She rushed into the shuttle bay and hit the remote start on the jumper she usually used. It purred to life and the activation sequence started. It took two minutes for the auto pilot to do safety checks and heat the engine. Hopefully Mr. Hot Bodyguard wouldn't make it out of his room before she'd taken off.

She stepped into the shuttle. But just in case he did… "Computer, close all the doors and go to full lock down."

"Affirmative." The deadpan, digital, female voice said.

"How long until you're able to fly?"

"One minute, thirty-six seconds."

She nodded. Good, he couldn't crack the door controls in that amount of time. "Set autopilot for the Haven District. Area five."

"Affirmative."

Now all she had to do was sit back and relax, and wait the thirty-eight minutes it took to get to the city.

"Passenger, Galen Marduk is asking for entrance. Should it be granted?"

There was a thump on the outside of the ship and it rocked slightly.

"Minor hull damage."

"What? Holy hell. What is that mad man doing?" That wasn't possible. He couldn't have dinged the ship with his fists.

"This vessel was kicked with an enforced boot. My readings show the culprit cannot be human. Possible hostile."

Damn right he was hostile. He damaged her jumper.

"Access granted."

"What? Computer, I didn't ask for anything."

The doors at the back of the shuttle started to lower. He must have managed to get them open. How was that possible? "Computer, override and close the doors."

"Access denied."

Fuck. What now? She had to go. People were counting on her. She had to get to the Haven District. Maybe he wouldn't be able to work his way into the piloting systems as quickly. She'd have to take him along for the ride.

"Computer, is the autopilot still set to the Haven District?"

"Affirmative."

"Good. Shut down all access to the piloting array until I say otherwise."

"Complete."

Galen stomped into the ship and the doors automatically closed behind him. "Computer, get those back open."

"Unable to comply, this shuttle is leaving the bay. The doors must stay closed. It is recommended that all occupants sit down and strap in."

Jamila grinned at him. "I'd do what the lady says. Liftoff in these old shuttles can be a bit rocky, but I think they're more reliable than the newer models. That old saying 'They don't make 'em like they used to' definitely applies."

"Computer, override the launch sequence."

"Unable to comply. Autopilot is set. The piloting array is offline until Jamila Christianna Clearborne reinitializes it."

Galen glared at Jamila like he was tempted to walk over and strangle her. "Dammit! Unlock the system, princess."

"Nope. I have something I have to do, and I intend to do it. I don't have a problem with you coming along for the ride. So sit down because—"

"Liftoff."

The force of the launch sent Galen tumbling to the back of the ship. He hit the doors with a loud clang and she flinched. If his boot could dent the hull, what could his whole body hitting the doors do? Luckily, they didn't fly open.

He groaned and rubbed the back of his head and she smirked at him. "Aren't you glad the doors close automatically for launch? You would have hit the floor of the bay awfully hard. Even *your* thick skull would have been damaged."

He stood, and clenched and released his fists a few times before he stomped toward her. She realized she had one pissed off man on her hands a second too late. He hit the release on her harness, grabbed her upper arms, and hauled her out of the seat.

"Well, at least this gives us a chance to chat. From now on, you're going to do as I say. I don't want to die doing this job. I know you're a little bitch, and you probably don't care what happens to me, but I'd like to keep breathing."

"I go out all the—"

"Don't interrupt me," he shouted over her. "I don't care what you normally do. I'm responsible for you now, and your father said to keep you out of trouble."

"I'm twenty-four. I don't need my daddy telling me what to do. I'm a grown woman."

"Then get a fucking job and leave so he can't boss you around anymore. Until then you're my problem."

He dropped her back into the chair and raked a hand through his hair. His words stung, even though they shouldn't. She didn't know him at all. It shouldn't matter if he thought she was his obligation and a spoiled little bitch. She was always someone's problem. Her father had just decided to pass his dilemma off to someone else.

She faced the console and checked the readouts for anything strange. He had kicked the shuttle and crashed into the doors, after all.

"Turn us around, Jamila."

She rolled her eyes but refused to look at him. "Nope."

• • •

Somehow Galen said something that upset her. He wasn't sure what part. Probably the bitch part. He was sure no one had ever dared call her a bitch before. He sighed in frustration. Keeping one little slip of a woman out of trouble shouldn't be this difficult. Didn't she realize the danger she was in? Apparently not, since the computer silently told him they were headed for the Haven District and probably the Forbidden District next to it, where her father was incredibly disliked. There had been riots on the streets over his possible reelection. To top it off, that was a dangerous area for anyone ever. It was violent on a daily basis, and not just because of recent riots. There were gangs, thieves, rapists, and murderers. And then a normal class of people who were down on their luck, and had to steal to keep food in their families' mouths.

He knew how dangerous it could be. He'd grown up in a place exactly like it. Everyone was doing something nefarious. There was a fine line between good and bad when your children were starving, and you couldn't get medical care for them. Life was hard. And when you put the daughter of the people's greatest enemy at their fingertips? Eventually Jamila's luck would run out.

But why would she go to the Haven District? Was she even allowed entrance? Some people were, but that was usually workers who had to pass through to get to their jobs.

Unfortunately, he had no choice but to go along. The computer wasn't recognizing his commands. He'd been silently trying to take the system back with his implants and it wasn't working. Well, he could keep her alive for one evening out. Her father was crazy if he thought he could keep her indoors all the time. However, Galen would have to try and keep her in the districts she was allowed in. Shopping and upscale clubs, not the rank bars her file said she frequented in Forbidden.

Why did she like going there, anyway? The bars she went to were likely holes in the wall and dirtier than a sewer. Plus, you could only get poor people drugs there. Surely she stuck to the prescription stuff. That had been her mother's downfall. But then, maybe she wanted to do anything to make her daddy crazy.

She still hadn't glanced at him. He sighed again and sat down. He didn't strap in quite yet. He'd been caught off guard when they'd taken off; he'd been too focused on her. This poor little ship wouldn't knock him on his ass if he were paying attention.

He rolled his shoulders. The silence was uncomfortable. He hadn't meant to upset her. He should have chosen his words more carefully. She already exhibited all the symptoms of depression. She lay in bed till all hours of the day, but she didn't sleep—instead she stared blankly at the ceiling. It was how he'd found her this morning, probably how she'd been when her father had called her to him to inspect the slaves. And even though she'd read most of the afternoon, he had caught her staring into space a few times.

Her file said she'd found her mother after she'd committed suicide. That must have done something to her. Before that she'd supposedly been the model of the perfect daughter, on her way to a high powered government job. She'd had her pick of colleges if she'd chosen to go. But he noticed she never smiled. In those pictures before her mother's suicide, she was as stoic as her father. After, at least she'd pretended to smile. Even if it never reached her eyes. In fact, he couldn't recall a single picture in her file where her smile lit her face. It was all pretend. He felt sorry for her. In spite of having a shit life, at least he'd had some happiness, before the government took it all away. Since then, all he'd seen was blood and death and a corrupt system that now wanted him, and everyone like him—those cyborgs they couldn't control—dead.

He took a deep breath. *That's right. Remember why you're here. Don't get sucked into this girl's problems. You have your own. You're trying to save lives. Ignore her.*

But he couldn't. Not entirely. "What did I say to upset you? I expected you to get pissed and even with me, not sulk."

She lifted her head and met his gaze. There was a flash of fire in her eyes and he couldn't fight down a surge of triumph. He couldn't stand it when he could cow people. He wanted her to fight back, even if it made his job that much harder. In spite of cyborgs being designed to subjugate people, they seemed to prefer it when people argued and fought back. Part of them always looked for a challenge—especially when it came to potential mate. Only people with fire would be any fun. It was probably more basic than that. Only tough women would create strong children. He restrained a growl. Dammit, he wasn't looking for a mate. He wasn't willing to risk his dick to possess her. She was needed to achieve their goals. That was all.

"I'm always an obligation for my father, but I don't give a damn what you think of me, Galen. I'm your job. It's your job to protect me. I'm the only thing you have to worry about aside from dying if you fail. I happen to have a life, and I intend to keep on living it no matter what you say or think. I'm not your problem. You might even earn your freedom if you'll stop bitching and keep me alive. Now shut up. I'd like to spend the rest of this journey in peace." She spat at him.

He arched an eyebrow as she buckled her harness, leaned back in her chair, and closed her eyes. So it hadn't been the bitch comment. Her outburst brought half a dozen questions to his mind. "Has your father really called you a burden?"

She frowned, but didn't open her eyes. "Yes. Many times. Me and Mother both. We weren't proper enough. No matter what my mother did, she couldn't please him. She had darker skin, and spoke with an accent she couldn't shake. She was born on Earth, you know? In a place they used to call Turkey. War destroyed all governments on Earth, but she'd still point out her country on an old map. She always said she would love to show me the ancient architecture. Some ruins still stand from those times. Or at least they were standing last time she was there. But I'll never see it. Earth is too dangerous now. And because of my father's constant complaining, she'll never see it again either."

Galen examined her. She still hadn't opened her eyes. In fact, they were squeezed tight. "You blame him for your mother's suicide." It was a statement, not a question. He could tell by her bitter tone.

"Of course I blame him. If she hadn't been such a 'burden' to him, with her thick accent and her different ways, she might have wanted to keep living. If he'd stood by her while the media judged her, she might have felt wanted. Apparently, the love of a daughter isn't enough. She needed her husband, and he failed her."

And she'd failed Jamila. That was how Galen saw it, anyway. She'd been weak, and left her daughter to endure a man who would never think she was good enough.

"And what does your father think of you?"

"My grades were never good enough. I was the highest ranking student at my boarding school, in all fields of study. But because I wasn't highest on the planet, he said I could still do better. I didn't get accepted to the one school he wanted me to go to. He hated that I did art. I danced, and drew. My mother said I was the best painter she'd seen, after her own father, and that one day I would surpass even him. And of course there are my looks. I'm too tall, too curvy and I'm the image of my mother with the exception of his ice blue eyes. And now? I will never do anything right ever again. Oh, I could turn my behavior around, but it would never fix me in his eyes."

Jamila was beautiful to him. How anyone could find her exotic appearance appalling was beyond him. "You said you did art? Past tense?"

"Yes. After I found her there was no beauty left in the world. I haven't bothered since. I haven't even felt the urge. When I go out to a club I go to drink, and have sex. I've danced a few times, but nothing like what I would do artistically."

There was a twinge in his chest. He felt sorry for this gorgeous, spoiled creature. A gilded cage. That was what she lived in. She couldn't be who her father wanted her to be. She couldn't go on being who her mother had wanted her to be. So she did what she could to piss off the last parent she had. She was a twenty-four-year-old woman going through a sixteen-year-old's rebellion. It should have sickened him, but she had her reasons.

"Oh, and Galen? That comment earlier about getting a job and moving away? I'm not allowed. The voters wouldn't like their senator's daughter working. Only the rich, well-bred families vote. My working would mean he doesn't make enough money to keep me in luxury. Besides, I'm supposed to marry, and produce children. A mother can't work. We've surpassed the age of space travel and gone right back to the fucking Dark Ages."

She was right, of course. Most well-bred women, though educated, still didn't have careers because everyone would assume their husbands couldn't keep them. Society saw no personal fulfillment in a woman having a career. She would never get out from under her father's thumb unless she married, and then she'd be oppressed by a husband. Some lily white dandy who was daintier than her. A man who wouldn't be fit to spit polish her shoes. Maybe Galen was doing her a favor. He almost laughed. She certainly wouldn't see it that way when all was said and done.

She finally opened her eyes and glanced his way. Her eyes were shiny, but no tears had escaped to spill down her cheeks. "Why am I telling you all this?"

He shrugged. "Maybe because I was the first person to ask."

She bit her lip and nodded. "Yes, no one has ever wanted to know anything about me. Most of my friends like me for my money, and enjoy pissing off their parents at least as much as I enjoy annoying my father."

He smiled. "Or maybe I made you so angry, you were willing to talk about anything to keep me quiet." It was bullshit. If angering her had any effect, it got her to drop her guard. He had a lot of information on her now. Information he'd probably use to hurt her. He hoped he would never have to.

She batted her lashes at him. "Well, Galen, we've talked so much about me. What about you? What deep, dark, tortured past lurks behind those blue peepers? What are your secrets?"

Galen shook his head. If she knew all the things he kept from her, she'd have him executed, along with the rest of his people. But could he reveal a small part of his past without giving her enough to get himself killed? Maybe. He hadn't shared it with many people. It wasn't something he liked to talk about. He considered his options. Her gaze seemed to plead with him to share something. She was vulnerable right now. She needed to connect. Maybe if he gave her something small, she would feel closer to him. It might make his job easier. Both his slavery and his actual mission.

He shrugged, trying for nonchalance. In reality the wounds he was about to reveal were nowhere near healed. And every moment he spent on this mission made them that much more raw.

"There isn't much to tell. I was in the military. When I came back, my wife claimed I'd changed, and it wasn't for the better. She left me. Took our daughter with her. I abandoned my post to search for them, and later was taken captive by the slave trader when I was caught stealing food in a district a lot like Forbidden. He knew I would make him good money. Granted, he was only supposed to deal cyborgs the government was willing to part with. He broke the law by selling me."

About eighty percent of that was a lie. She'd never notice. Cyborgs were the government's dirty little secret. People knew they were created, but not for what purposes and against their will. He'd been trained to lie with almost no signs—only another one of his kind would have been able to tell that he was bullshitting. He hadn't been in the military. He'd been trained by their government, and was better than your average soldier. He'd never looked for his wife until much later in life. He'd been kidnapped by people like him, and deprogrammed. He was a thief to be sure. Since his deprogramming, he'd stolen food, medical supplies, fuel, the government's deep dark secrets they didn't want anyone to know about…but it hadn't landed him here. He'd deliberately placed himself with that slaver.

The only part he hadn't twisted was his wife and daughter leaving him, and the reason why. He hadn't even known she was pregnant when he'd been taken. She hadn't gotten the nerve to tell him yet. Having a baby wasn't a good thing. They couldn't have gotten medical care for either of them, and it was another mouth to feed.

But it didn't matter. He would never know his daughter and never had to take care of her. He hadn't been worried about his wife once they'd fucked up his mind. He'd been changed, and when he was sent back to her, he'd been sickeningly loyal to the government. He'd also been aggressive, dominant, dangerous... He could see every little lie she told, and she'd held some pretty damning secrets of her own.

He shook himself. He didn't want to dwell on his wife leaving him. At the time, it hadn't mattered. Nothing but serving the Federation of Planets had mattered. Now, thinking about it hurt. As soon as he'd been able to remember who he was, he'd been in physical pain from his loss. No matter how hard he'd tried, he never could find Amanda, or baby Charlise, who would be far from a child by now. At twenty-seven, she would look more like his sister than his daughter. He hadn't aged since the government had accelerated his growth. None of them had. They didn't know if it was a kind of immortality due to genetic alterations, or if one day their time would run out, and they were just being kept in fighting form.

"It sounds like you could add a lot more to that." Jamila glanced at him.

"I'm sure you could add a lot more to the story of your mother's suicide, but you aren't going to. You can't bear it. And I really don't want to tell the story of how my shitty life managed to go down the toilet."

She bit her lip. "I'm sorry about your wife and kid. I've only ever lost a mother. I can't imagine losing a child, or the person I loved."

He stared at her for a second. He couldn't believe what he was hearing. She was actually showing him compassion. It was sincere. It filled her eyes with a sad light, and the slight sheen of tears.

Tears for him, a man she seemed to despise, and a woman and child she'd never met.

She laid her hand over his and squeezed.

He smiled politely, because he didn't know what to do. "Thank you."

Chapter Three

"Approaching destination."

Jamila straightened and braced herself for the landing. "Strap in, Galen. I'd hate for you to hit that hard head of yours again."

The little vessel dipped sharply as it came in for a landing. Nothing slow and controlled for this old beast. Maybe that was why she liked it. It was a little wild and dangerous. Something she admired in all things. Galen strapped himself in and gripped the arm rests until his knuckles turned white.

"What's wrong, Galen? You look nervous."

He glared at her. "I'm not the biggest fan of in-planet flying, and I've never felt a ship hurtle toward earth quite like this. Are you sure something isn't wrong?"

She grinned. "If it is, I blame you. You kicked my jumper, after all."

"From now on we're taking a new model everywhere we go, and I want to pilot. I fucking hate autopilot."

"Autopilot is more reliable than a human, with faster reaction time."

He snorted and muttered under his breath, "It's not faster than my reaction time."

She turned her attention to the consoles in front of her to hide her shock. Was he really faster than computer response times? They said cyborgs had computers enhancing their brains. Maybe he could be as good. She shook her head. No, not possible. He was good, but no one was that good.

The ship jerked as the thrusters came on to slow their descent. The curves of the muscles of Galen's arms stood out in stark relief, so tense that he might snap in half when they finally landed. She might have laughed if his mouth wasn't creased in a stern frown. The small vessel touched the ground, throwing them against their harnesses.

"Now will you turn us around and take us back to your home?"

She glanced at him to find him glaring at her and laughed. "I'd think you'd want to get out of this cursed thing for a while, and build up some courage for the trip back."

His stern glower made her giggle. "That would be a nice thought, if I wasn't worried about your safety. I don't want you getting killed."

Her good humor left her. "I'm not five. I've been coming out here for six months and the Forbidden District for even longer. Nothing bad has ever happened." Well, that wasn't entirely true. She'd had some close calls over the years, but her friends had always been there to back her up. But she wasn't going to tell him that.

"Ah. I've caught you in a lie. There's something you're not telling me, Jamila."

She rolled her eyes. Of course he could tell she was lying. "It's nothing. Don't worry your pretty little head about it. If you're that concerned for our safety, you can stay here. You'll be nice and safe in this shuttle."

"You know I have no care for my own safety. I can and have healed many severe injuries."

"And with medical help, I can too. And since we have the best medical care on the planet, I'm not worried."

He growled at her as he removed his harness. She shrugged out of hers and stood, before he could do something to prevent her.

"Like I told you, Galen, I have things to do. And then I plan to see my friends, with you as a big, scowling shadow at my back."

Honestly, she'd given up the idea of meeting her friends. She wanted to make sure the people who were counting on her got what they needed, but hearing his grumble over every little thing made her want to mess with his head a little.

She walked to the back of the shuttle and pulled the bags from the overhead compartment. She'd gotten her packages stashed before Galen was purchased.

"As long as you're standing here growling at me, why don't you make yourself useful and grab a couple bags. Please be careful with them, some of the stuff is fragile."

He lifted the heaviest bag like it weighed nothing. She'd had to wheel it in here with an anti-grav unit, and it had taken two pilots to stow it in the overhead compartments. She closed her gaping mouth and started to collect the other bags.

"What's in this? It weighs a hundred and two point five pounds."

He could tell exactly how much it weighed? He must have some weird sensors tied up in his brain.

"You'll see what it is in about thirty minutes. We've got a long walk ahead of us. If that bag is too much, I can get the anti-gravity transport."

He shook his head. "It's fine, an anti-grav unit will slow us down. As long as I keep one arm free, I'll be okay."

He was right; it would slow them down. Was he carrying a weapon? Was that why he needed one arm free? She hoped not. People tended to go nuts in Haven when they saw weapons. There seemed to be some worry that the government would send in undercover operatives to wipe out the population. That they might one day open fire and slaughter everyone. There were whispers that it had been done before. Jamila always rolled her eyes at the stories. The government had its faults, but it wasn't slaughtering innocent people.

"Computer, open the doors."

It complied with no hesitation. She grabbed the three remaining lighter bags and walked down the ramp, Galen following almost too close for comfort. Did he not know the meaning of the term "personal space"?

She walked toward the center of town. Haven was bustling with people in spite of the bitterly cold weather. Jamila kept getting strange, frightened glances as they passed. Many smiled and met her gaze, but when they spotted Galen their eyes darted to the side as they shuffled past. She hardly drew any attention these days. She was here once a week bringing her care packages. Occasionally the people helped her carry things.

She glanced at Galen. He glowered at every person who dared to look at her. She stopped and he came to a halt behind her.

"You're scaring the crap out of these people. You could smile and nod instead of glare, and if you can't manage that you could stare at the ground."

"I want them scared. I want them to think twice before approaching you. And I can't look down, I'm guarding you."

"I don't mind if these people approach me. Many of them do if they need help with something. Try not to glower."

He gave her a blank faced stare, his eyes losing all heated intensity. "Will this do?"

She rolled her eyes. "Next time I'm tying you up and leaving you at home."

He muttered under his breath, "Maybe next time I'm tying you to your bed where I can have a little fun and you won't be at risk of getting killed."

She gaped at him. "What did you say?"

He smirked. "You heard me. I'm not going to repeat it. I'll be in even more trouble than I am already, judging by the tick at the corner of your mouth and the murderous look in your eyes."

She spun around and stomped off toward their destination. Tie her to the bed? How dare he. *Oh, come on, you're so offended because the thought really turned you on.*

She slowed her stride. Yeah, it had. She wasn't a girl who wanted to be tied up. She'd been horrified by the things she'd done when she was abusing drugs and booze after she'd gotten clean. Things she didn't remember doing. She never planned to give up control again, in any way. And being at a cyborg's mercy wasn't a good plan.

She shook her head and picked up her pace again. She didn't need to glance over her shoulder to know that he kept up with her. She couldn't have him. He was dangerous.

He'd been genetically altered and his bones and joints were reinforced. Would he go crazy like other genetically engineered people sometimes did? Not long after she'd been born, one had lost his mind, believing he was superior to normal humans, and set out to take over the government. He'd killed a lot of people, and managed to assassinate the Ascendant before they'd captured him and put him and his followers to death.

That had led to the Genetic Purity Movement, and a mass genocide of everyone who had even the tiniest alteration. Eventually they'd stopped due to public outrage. A lot of those people were innocent, productive members of society. So instead, they'd started putting them in Haven districts, like the one they were in now.

They were supposed to be protected and taken care of, but not allowed to pass on their altered genes. Instead they lived in squalor, and were fed slop that dogs wouldn't eat. They weren't allowed outside of their districts or to travel off world. They couldn't have jobs. Housing was overcrowded so some didn't even have roofs over their heads.

She glanced around. A lot of these people were deeply unhappy. Drinking and drugs were prevalent, but they'd rarely been cruel to her, especially when they'd learned that she was trying to help them.

They turned down Meadow Lane when three children ran by in a rush of laugher. The last one, Jackson, stumbled to a halt. "Miss Clearborne!" He ran headlong into her and threw his thin arms around her hips.

"Ooof! Hey, Jackson. You're getting too big for that. You almost took me down." She ruffled his baby-fine blond hair as he stepped back. "Where is Alice?"

"She's inside fighting with Darion." He lowered his voice. "Darion's been sneaking out of the zone to steal again, and Alice is worried she'll be killed if she's caught."

Fear clenched her stomach and she crouched down next to Jackson. "Does anyone else know about this?"

He nodded. "A few of the other kids heard them fighting."

She took a deep breath. "Okay, make sure they don't tell anyone. No one can know. Not even people within the district. Do you understand? It's important."

He bit his lip. "I'll tell them, but they're kids. They might not remember. And lots of them aren't good at lying."

She grinned. "I know, just tell them. Now get out of here and go play."

Her false smile dropped as he rushed past her, screaming for the other children to wait for him. She rolled her shoulders as she stood, trying to get rid of the tension. She had to talk to Darion.

Striding through the open front door, Jamila didn't bother to announce herself. She walked into the kitchen and grinned when she spotted Darion lip-locked with Alice, her tan hands wrapped in Alice's blond hair.

She cleared her throat. "I thought you were fighting?"

Alice flushed as she pulled away. "We are." She spotted Galen and frowned. "Who is that?"

Jamila ignored her and wiggled her eyebrows. "Getting to the make-up part?"

Alice glared at Darion, and crossed her arms over her chest. "No, we're not."

"Great, because I'm about to start the argument again. Darion, you can't leave the Zone. You're risking your life if you're caught, and Alice's. Surely that means something to you, even if risking yourself doesn't. Who will take care of these orphans if you aren't around?"

Darion threw her arms in the air. "Who's taking care of them now? We have no food. We can't educate them because we have no books. We can't fix this rat trap, piece of shit house. They'd do just as well on the streets."

Jamila shook her head. "That's not true and you know it. Tell me what you need. Give me a list. I'll get it. I've brought food, basic supplies, and medication for the Sobasus."

Alice sagged against the counter. "Oh, thank the gods for you, Jamila. We have two children who are desperately ill. We were certain they would die."

Sobasus was fatal if it wasn't treated. It was very common in the slums and Haven districts, where people couldn't get meds. It was also very contagious. Before the drugs had been invented for it, it had killed off entire planets of people. She hoped they'd kept those two kids quarantined once they'd found out. If other people in the zone caught it, it would spread like wildfire. It was one of the few illnesses genetically engineered people were capable of catching.

Jamila nodded. "I took enough to treat fifteen cases. I can get more, but only about the same amount at one time. I've also brought food and a few water condenser canteens as well as a filtration system, if you're given water."

Galen slipped past her and relieved her of the other bags. He opened them and raked his hands through his hair before bracing them on the counter. What was he thinking? She couldn't see his face, but his body language said she might be in trouble.

Darion stared at his back for a second before she shook her head and turned back to Jamila. "This is my point. I love you, Jamila, but a woman should be able to support her family on her own. She shouldn't have to rely on charity of others."

"This is an orphanage, not strictly your family. Even if you could get a job, you'd need help. And it's not charity. You've been wronged. This is the least I can do until it's put right."

Unfortunately, her arguments with her father about how these people were treated never went well. He remembered the Genetic Purity Movement and the events that led to it. He'd been friends with the assassinated Ascendant and several senators who'd been killed. He believed he was right, and that made it so much harder to convince him of anything.

Alice nudged Jamila with her elbow. "So really, who is Mr. Tall-Hot-and-Silent?"

"Bodyguard. Galen."

She grinned. "Does he do a good job guarding your body? If you know what I mean."

Jamila rolled her eyes. "The walls know what you mean. We haven't done that. He's a stubborn pain in the ass."

Darion nudged her. "But I bet he's good in bed. You should get under him. Might help you get over that Crougar guy."

Jamila sighed. "There's nothing to get over. He was a pompous douche bag, and I drove him off."

And promptly told her father that if he ever tried to get her to marry another man like Crougar, she'd do something much worse to him. There'd been a big, loud fight over that.

"Either way. I think you should jump Mr. Bodyguard."

She shook her head. "No, thank you. He thinks I'm a spoiled little bitch. And he's controlling. Hotness only gets you so far. He's also dangerous."

Darion and Alice glanced at each other. "Because he's one of us?"

Jamila wasn't surprised that they recognized him as genetically engineered. But did they realize he was a cyborg?

"He's not one of you."

Darion rolled her eyes. "Even our friend fears people like us, Alice."

"Darion, that's not how it is."

Galen finally turned to me, his face unreadable. "How is it then?"

She glared at him. "I don't know you, and so far I think you're a pain in my ass."

He leaned back against the counter and crossed his ankles. "Because you know the other men you sleep with so well."

She stared at the ceiling and counted to ten, hoping for patience so she wouldn't beat him over the head. "You're an admitted criminal. You're also a cyborg. Different from being plain old gen engineered. And no, maybe I don't know every man I sleep with, but the difference is, if it came down to a fight, I could probably take them, or at least hurt them enough to get them to back off. With you I'm screwed if you plan to hurt me."

He snorted. "You could get me executed."

"Not before you killed me."

"We're linked. You die, I die, honey."

She crossed her arms over her chest. "And how do I know you haven't found a way to overcome that? I saw how you took over my little ship. There was no other way you could have gotten it open. You have some kind of communication going on with electronics. I'm guessing you could break your servant bonds."

"If I could, I would have. I haven't managed it so far. They must be more advanced than what I was trained with." He pulled out a vial of Medicrom 10 and handed it and a syringe to Alice. "You ladies should probably go dose those kids. Sodasus claims its victims quickly."

Alice took the bottle from him and turned to leave. When she reached Jamila, she patted her arm. "Thank you so much. I hope it's not too much trouble for you to get this stuff."

"You're welcome. It's no trouble. I've got connections." She wouldn't dare tell Alice or Darion the truth. They both left to go tend to the sickly kids.

"You're a great liar."

She kept her expression blank and glanced at him. "I don't know what you mean."

He advanced on her and she ignored the urge to back up. "Yes, you do. You know giving medical supplies to the genetically altered is illegal. The government decides what they can and can't have. They would never give them Medicrom 10. They don't care about this place. They left these people to die. They want the population gone. These people are expected to treat their own illnesses. You're likely to be executed or at least severely punished if you're found out. Why do it?"

She took a deep breath. "Okay, I'll tell you a story. One night I was partying with my girlfriends when Jackson, the little boy who ran into me outside, took my purse. He was so small I figured I could catch him. I figured he was some little urchin who lived in Forbidden. When he crawled under the wall into the zone, I went right after him. I was drunk and didn't realize where I was going, or that he shouldn't have been outside of this place. I had some snacks and water in my purse, because you don't eat or drink anything in Forbidden unless it comes right from the bartender. There's a large risk of being drugged, or catching an illness from the food. He must have seen me eating. When I crossed the wall, I discovered that he'd tossed my ident cards, which would have given him access to my accounts if he'd gotten my fingerprints, and since he had my bag, he also had prints. I followed him here. He went into the back of the building and when I rounded the corner, he was handing out food and the water bottle was being passed around. All the children were so thin and frail, like they hadn't eaten in months."

She raked a hand through her hair. "Darion stepped out, and asked where he'd gotten the food. He wouldn't tell her. And then she spotted me. She all but cowed before me, when I told her what the boy had done. She begged me not to turn him in. That powerful bitch you met today, who braves execution, and she begged me. I could tell she wasn't used to doing that. I knew they'd all be killed if even one was found sneaking to the other side of the wall, and I couldn't stand how sickly everyone appeared. So the next day I grabbed the codes my father has for the zone so I could land here. I brought food and water, some of my old clothes, anything I could think of that they might need, and I came back. And I haven't stopped. It quickly went from bringing them food to stealing medical supplies when the Sodasus struck the first time. What was I supposed to do? What would anyone do?"

He stared at her for a full minute before he spoke. "Most people would have left them. Turned that boy in, and never looked back. They're genetically engineered. They could be insane."

"They're just children whose parents made the mistake of having them altered for God knows what reason. What if they were ill or something? You don't know. They're innocent. And I've only seen two cases of insanity while I've been here, and you know what? I was saved by people like them. So don't tell me—"

He grabbed her upper arms and hauled her against him. His lips brushed hers in a gentle kiss. "I think you're incredible. You could have made them suffer."

He pressed his mouth against hers again, tangling his hands in her hair. His tongue took advantage of her open mouth, dueling with hers. She leaned into him, sliding her palms around his waist. He tasted like rich, creamy coffee, something he seemed to drink by the pot.

He backed up, clutching the curve of her ass. Her butt bumped the counter and he lifted her, placing her on it. He wedged his hips between her thighs and ran his hands under her blouse to skim her ribs, but he went no higher, teasing her. She wrapped her legs around his hips and tugged him closer. His erection ground against her clit and she moaned as she rubbed against him.

There was loud thump upstairs and she jumped and pulled away reluctantly, dazed. "We shouldn't be doing this."

He grinned. "Yes, we should. Though here isn't the best place. I'm sure they can hear us. The thump was probably a deliberate warning. You've done something extraordinary. Something I haven't seen a lot of normal people do. They hate us. Think we're dangerous. And most of these people aren't nearly as dangerous as I am. They're innocent, like you said."

"So you admit you're dangerous?"

He arched an eyebrow. "Yes, I can't possibly deny that. It's obvious. I have slaves' barcodes and cybernetic enhancements out the ass. You would know I was lying if I said I wasn't."

Chapter Four

She stared at him for a minute. He took in her beauty. He regretted what he'd have to do now. He might make an enemy of this woman for these people. It was a sobering thought. No, he would do his damnedest not to let that happen. He would have to explain to her. She would understand. He flinched internally. Then again, she might not.

She surprised him. She was a compassionate woman. It was amazing, since she was the spoiled, rich daughter of a senator who hated his kind.

She cleared her throat and hopped off the counter, avoiding his gaze. "We need to go. My father expects me at dinner and I still have to get something from Forbidden."

"What?" He narrowed his eyes, immediately suspicious. He was supposed to keep her from partying there. It was also rumored that she did a lot of drugs, which she could easily get in that district.

She shrugged and walked away from him. "Stuff."

He grabbed her arm and jerked her to a stop. "I want you to tell me. You're too good to be out there. It's dangerous, and I refuse to go if you're going to get high and drink."

She glared at him and tugged her arm out of his grip. He let her go. He could have kept his hold on her. "It's nothing like that. I haven't been doing either of those things in a long while."

"Then what is it?"

"It's food, alright? For these people. I have to get them food bricks. I can't get them anything that goes bad. But I couldn't possibly get enough bricks to feed everyone through usual channels. I don't think we even have them at our house. They taste like shit. They're strictly everything you need to live, with no regard for flavor. The rich don't eat them. So I had to get them from someone else. I have to meet my contact in fifteen minutes, and he gets antsy if I'm late. He assumes I'm doing something illegal if I'm getting them from him. Luckily, he's thought of everything but what I'm actually doing. I trust him enough to get me the food, but definitely not enough to tell him."

He snorted. "Yeah, that's probably for the best. If he's getting it for you, he's doing it illegally. Can't trust criminals."

She eyed him. "So I shouldn't trust you?"

He shrugged. "I'm not your average criminal. I went to prison more for what I am, not what I did. It's a little different."

Except that she definitely shouldn't trust him. He couldn't hint at that, though. He had to make sure she felt she had nothing to fear.

He nodded. "Lead the way. I'll trust your judgment this time."

She smiled at him like it meant the world to her that he trusted her. Honestly, he didn't. She didn't know how dangerous the world was. She had no idea how much trouble she was in. Though he suspected her father kept her too sheltered. She led him around the house to the fence and stood before a small hole. She bit her lip and glanced at him.

"I don't know if you'll fit. I barely do, and I'm quite a bit smaller than you. The fence is electrified so you can't climb it and there are spikes on the top. If you would stay here, I'll be—"

"No. End of discussion. Not happening. We'll find a way." He glanced around and spotted what he was searching for. The small grid that maintained this part of the fence. He walked over to it and accessed the computer that maintained it with his mind. *Oh, that was too easy.* He could only take it out for five minutes tops but he could almost jump this fence, so he wouldn't be pressed for time.

"Don't go under the fence until I'm over it."

"But how—"

He shrugged off his jacket and threw it over the spikes at the top of the fence as he shut down the power. The slight humming stopped abruptly. He jumped, landing under the spikes, careful not to land on them.

He crawled over the barbs. If he slipped, he'd kill himself. Luckily, he was barely human anymore. He was unlikely to lose his footing. The sharp tips pricked his hands, and blood spread across his jacket. He shut down the pain receptors in his brain as he crossed. Unfortunately, it was only a temporary reprieve. Eventually he wouldn't be able to shut out the injury. Luckily, they should be healed by then. He landed on his feet on the other side, pulling his jacket with him.

"Hurry and crawl under there. The electricity is off, but it won't be for long. I'd rather you get over here before its back on. No matter how many times you've made it through without touching the barrier." He shuddered at the thought. If she touched that fence, it would probably kill her. He reset the strength of the shock while he had control of the system. The reduced level would knock a person out now, but not kill them. It would only last until they updated things. He covered his tracks to make it appear like some sort of power failure had reset it. With the rough weather Larus was having this winter, they wouldn't double check it.

Jamila pushed her bag through the hole before her arms and head appeared under the barricade. A ringing in his ears told him the fence's grid was rebooting. He grabbed her arms and tugged her out.

She stumbled into him with a gasp. "You know, if the electricity came back on, I would have had a better shot climbing out myself and not getting shocked then to have you pull me out."

He rolled his eyes. "No, you wouldn't have. Did you touch it at all when I pulled you out?"

She glanced at the ground, and her jaw clenched. "No."

"That's right. Now let's get out of here before someone spots us. By the way, how are we going to get back to the ship? I have no desire to climb that again."

"Why, it seemed to go smoothly?"

"This security system learns. Next time I hack it, we'll have less time to get over. Besides, scaling that thing isn't without its price."

"What do you mean?"

They came to the mouth of the alley and he looked both ways, hoping no patrollers were roaming around. He flashed his palm at her absentmindedly as he observed the area for threats. There was a throng of people waiting outside the club that they could disappear into.

"Oh, Galen. Why didn't you say something?"

He grunted. "Doesn't matter. Can't feel it. I managed to get over the wall anyway."

He lowered his hand and she snatched it. "Wait. Let me bandage this, give me your other hand."

She pulled him around and grasped his other wrist to examine him. The worry on her face surprised him.

"Don't worry about it. If you bandage it, they'll seem suspicious this close to the border. Besides, it's not like the barbs went through my hand. I heal fast enough. The bleeding is already slowing."

"At least let me wipe off the blood."

He sighed. "In a second. We need to get farther away from this alley."

He grabbed her arm and hauled her out of it and down the street between the groups of people waiting to get inside the bar. He released her wrist, wiped his hands on his jacket, and tossed it in a garbage incinerator.

"Where to now, Jamila?"

She nodded and grasped his hand, entwining her fingers gently with his.

He leaned down the whisper in her ear. "You never answered me about getting back. Are you going to cross that wall again?"

Reaching into her pocket she pulled out a remote, and hit a blue button on it. "Nope. Since I reprogramed my ship, it's actually gotten much easier to get out of the zone than to get into it on foot. Unmanned vessels sometimes go to and from Haven delivering the scant amount of supplies they're allowed. The government won't look twice when mine joins us in the Forbidden district. It's also not safe to be in the zone after dark."

"It's not safe to be *here* after dark. In fact, it's probably more dangerous."

"Either way, I've started picking up next week's food supply after I drop off. This is the only time he'll meet with me and when my father is in town it's the only day I can get away."

He laughed. "I didn't know the old model ship had a remote calling option."

She grinned. "I had it installed."

He arched an eyebrow. "Why go through all that work to make an old ship do that when you could borrow a newer model?"

She snorted. "I do hope you've been out of contact with civilization for a while. Otherwise there's no dismissing your ignorance. Newer models are outfitted so they can't fly into the zone. It seems I'm not the only one helping these people, and when the government found out they created them with certain no fly zones built in. And if you over ride that, the authorities are alerted. I did a little research before I started flying into Haven because I'd heard of people being caught doing it. I've taken every precaution I can think of not to be caught."

She chewed her bottom lip. "But it's only a matter of time before the government demands all vehicles be updated with the new protocols. I don't know what they'll do then."

"I wasn't aware that the government was doing that to ships." His people didn't exactly have the latest intel on ship building. They were more focused on other things. He'd have to remedy that. These ships were probably made with other features that could be a problem for them if they stole a newer model.

"Oh yes, and it wasn't easy to find out because of all the censorship and spying. Luckily, I do remember something of my academy days in hacking, and was able to get a five minute private conversation with someone. Yay for government training."

The only problem with that was no conversation was private over the communications network. They were all stored. She'd have to remember more than a little hacking to get around that problem. Either he'd underestimated her, or she'd left something behind. He would bet on the latter. Most citizens didn't know exactly how much they were tracked by the government. How little privacy they had left. They'd probably protest if they had any idea. Even a government employee would have a little tidbit of knowledge withheld so their employers could keep tabs on them.

They ducked into another alley and she hesitated. She glanced at him over her shoulder. "I always hate this spot. I've been attacked here before. It's not the best of neighborhoods."

He smiled, but he was worried. There wasn't a streetlight back here. The place was steeped in darkness. "I've got your back. No mugger can get by me." He silently adjusted his eyes for night vision.

She jumped. "Your eyes. They're glowing now."

"Yep, sure are. Keep moving."

She shook her head, but kept walking. "Eventually, you're going to have to tell me the extent of your super powers."

"I don't have super powers." He kept pace with her now instead of letting her walk ahead of him. Guarding her in this place was really a two person job. Thankfully, he wasn't normal. He had enough censors that he could spot anything coming.

"He waits for me right around this corner."

Galen nodded, and they stepped around it. A robed man stood perfectly still in the middle of the lane. Galen pulled his pistol from its holster. Something thumped to the ground in front of the robed figure. Galen's gaze zeroed in on it and magnified enough to identify a grenade.

"Fuck! Run."

There was flash, and an energy blast struck him in shoulder. Jamila screamed as he shoved her back around the corner. He grabbed her under the arm and hauled her down the street. There was a faint click. He cursed and threw himself on top of her. They hit the ground hard, her gasp loud in his ears.

The explosion shook the ground. He covered his head as shrapnel rained from the sky and heat licked his skin. Jamila cried out, but he couldn't do anything except try to keep her covered as everything was sent into chaos.

They lay in silence for a second while he listened for movement. He sat up and checked on Jamila. Her lips were moving but he couldn't hear a word she said. A loud ringing filled his ears. He wouldn't be able to hear any threat coming at them. Fuck.

He pulled her to her feet and she screamed. Even through the damage to his ears he heard it faintly. She gestured to her leg. There was a piece of metal in her thigh. Dammit. What now? He couldn't pull it out here. Even if it hadn't hit an artery, it would bleed a hell of a lot. He didn't know where her ship was, so he couldn't take her to it.

They had to leave here. If he went the wrong way they could double back later, but they needed to move before the explosion attracted officers. Or the people who'd tried to kill her came after them again. He scanned the area but there was no sign of them. But that didn't mean they weren't there, or that they didn't have another trap set. He ducked, grabbed her around the knees, and tossed her over his shoulder, doing his best to ignore the blinding pain the movement caused. He stumbled and went down to his knees. He took a deep breath and tried to shut down the pain receptors in his brain, but things were too scrambled at the moment. The grenade must have stunned some of his systems.

He shoved himself to his feet and ran. Jamila's hands dug into his hips with such ferocity it was almost painful. He needed to get her some place where he could see to her wound. She wasn't bleeding much yet, but when he removed the spike, they'd see exactly what kind of problem they had.

He hesitated at the mouth of the alley. If they were spotted by patrollers they'd likely be arrested. Jamila hit his back repeatedly and he stopped. She was trying to tell him something. She tapped his left side, and he went that way. Hopefully that was what she meant. He stuck close to the buildings. Thankfully they were heading away from the crowds of downtown. She thumped his back again and he stopped.

When she tapped the right side of his body, he rushed across the street to the alley he spotted. He saw her ship at the end of it. He hacked the system as he jogged toward it. The doors opened slowly, the plank lowering to the ground so he could walk in.

"Tell the ship to start and get us the hell out of here." He sighed in relief. His hearing was coming back. He'd been worried for a second that it wouldn't. The sound of her telling the ship to take off reached his ears. Barely.

He crouched and set her feet on the ground. She stumbled a little and he grabbed her hips to steady her as he stood. Her tan complexion had become frighteningly pale.

Grasping her elbow, he guided her to the padded bench in the back of the shuttle. "Lie down. Is there a med kit in here?"

Her eyes narrowed, proof that she couldn't hear well either at the moment. He repeated his question and she nodded, pointing to the small cargo space on the opposite side of the shuttle. When he located the tiny kit he groaned. Nothing this small was going to be a lot of help.

He popped it open. The cell regenerator in here was probably only big enough to partially heal her wound. The pain injector was the big surprise. Apparently this med kit had been altered. They usually came with a standard painkiller. This had one that would make a person loopy as hell. Which was actually nice for his purposes. From the short view he'd gotten of her injury in the alley, it was pretty bad. He removed the mini doper machine from its sterile package and loaded it with the painkiller. He turned and pressed it to her arm. It automatically went off. Almost immediately she let her head rest on the bench.

"Wow, what was that? Usually the drugs in those kits are nothing. Whatever you gave me wasn't nothing."

"It was Vicaquian. One of the strongest painkillers you can get these days. Heavily abused though. I was shocked that it was in this med kit too. It's illegal to have such a powerful drug in them. Guess your daddy doesn't care much for legality."

"He's not a drug user if that's what you're implying."

"I'd never dream of saying that." Oh, yes he would. He suspected her father had many faults. Habitual drug use wouldn't surprise him. It was something almost every nobleman did. And in the government you had easy access.

"Yes, you would. You have no problem accusing anyone of horrible things. Even if you don't accuse, you definitely think it."

He moved to examine her leg, pulling a knife from his boot. He cut away her blood soaked pant leg around the injury, jostling the sliver of metal. "Does that hurt?"

"Are you kidding? I can't feel anything, anywhere. Disconcerting feeling."

"Oh, come now. I know you're a drug user, even if dear daddy isn't."

"Was a drug user. And I didn't do anything quite like this."

"What's so different about it?" He needed to keep her talking. He'd let her talk about anything.

"Most of the drugs me and my friends used created a euphoric feeling, not a numb body feeling."

"Not an orgasm feeling?"

She laughed. "Okay, so you caught me. I was a big user of that particular drug."

"Couldn't find anyone to get you off the good old fashioned way?"

She snickered. "Sometimes. I've met a lot of skeevy men and most of the time you don't want to sleep with any of them. Much better to take a drug that gets you off, and avoid the assholes that are out there."

"Or you could marry."

She snorted and shook her head. "Not you too? If my father brings in one more dickwad of a suitor, you'll have quite the murder-suicide on your hands. Those are the biggest assholes of them all. They're all rich, and political up and comers. Condescending, like I don't have a brain when, if I'd finished my schooling, I probably would have beaten them out of whatever position they hold."

"I have no doubt. Okay, I'm going to pull this out now." He didn't think the shard had hit an artery. She probably would have died already if it had, but it still was going to bleed a lot, and she'd already lost enough blood. The regenerator would probably only stop the blood loss.

He freed the shrapnel and blood immediately welled and started streaming down the sides of her leg onto the bench. He grabbed the regenerator and held it over her wound. The blood loss slowed and then stopped, but the batteries died before he was finished. He wiped away the blood, and was satisfied that the injury was no longer life threatening. He reloaded the doper with an antibiotic and injected it near the wound.

"There we go. That should do until we get you home and I can take you to medical."

"No! My father can't know about this outing, for your sake and mine. If he knows I was injured, he'll see it as your failure, and have you killed." She slowly sat up. She blinked hard and swayed.

"Maybe you should lie back down."

"I'm fine." She grabbed his arm. "You can't tell my father what happened, or anyone in the infirmary. Go get more medical supplies and fix the rest of my wound, but you can't take me to sick bay."

She eyed him but her gaze was unfocused. "I know you were hit. You should have used some of that on you."

He glanced at his shoulder. Blood had spread down his torso and was soaking into his pants. "It's nothing. I'm already healing. I do need to pull the cloth away from it though." He plucked it away from the wound and flinched.

"It's the gift of being what I am. You heal pretty damned fast." He whipped his shirt over his head and used it to wipe off the majority of blood that had spilled.

"We still need to give you a dose of antibiotics and see if we can't bandage it at least."

He showed her his palm, with the rapidly healing tiny puncture wounds. "Don't worry about me. See how these are healing? I'll be fine. I'm worried about you. It's very hard for me to catch an infection, but you'd be easily killed by one. My superior genetics can fight most things off."

"My God. Those look like they're days old."

He nodded. "Exactly."

"Launch imminent," the computer said. "Strap in."

Jamila pushed herself to sitting. "We need to move."

"No, stay here and brace yourself. We'll be okay."

He put his arm around her from his kneeling position on the floor and waited for liftoff. It wouldn't catch him off guard this time. The ship launched and he barely moved a muscle. Jamila shifted slightly, but kept her seat.

"Wow, you're so strong."

He grinned. "Yes, I am. How are you doing?"

"I'm okay. I think the bad parts of the painkiller are starting to wear off. I feel more focused than I was a second ago."

"Good. I need you to tell me what I should say to your father when you don't come to dinner."

"What time is it?"

"Almost nine."

"Crap, we're already late for dinner. We should make it back before he's done. We have to think of a lie about where we've been. How about shopping?"

"We don't have anything new."

She rolled her eyes. "Pfft, as long as he doesn't see us sneaking in, he'll never even ask what I bought. He doesn't care, as long as I'm not out creating a new scandal."

"Okay then. We were shopping and ate out."

She was still too pale for his liking. He got the feeling that if she sat up, she'd fall right back over. Would she need a transfusion? He glanced at the blood on her clothes and beneath her on the bench and made an estimate of what she'd lost. No, she would be fine without a transfusion. Weak, but she'd live. She wasn't cold to the touch, or shivering, and since he'd stopped the blood loss she would be fine. He tried to keep himself from worrying. Why the fuck was he concerned? She was a means to an end. Nothing more. But she was also beautiful, compassionate, and brave. She wouldn't be risking herself if she weren't.

"Does anyone know you meet this man?"

"Only Alice and Darion. They would never tell."

"Has anyone seen you meeting with him?"

She glared at him as best she could while lying on a bench. "No, why do you think we meet there?"

He rolled his eyes. "Well, either someone saw you or he betrayed you. Which do you think it is?"

She sighed. "Someone probably spotted us. He was doing something illegal too, so I doubt he ratted me out. Who do you think the assassins were?"

He snorted. "I don't know. I assume they're trying to kill you to strike at your father. I think if it were the government, they would have come out and arrested you. You're an important person. If they wanted to out you, they'd want to do it publically to make a point that even the upper classes won't get away with what you're doing."

"You know your life is great when you're happy it was a normal assassin and not the government."

"Yep."

"Approaching destination," the computer's robotic voice crackled. "Fasten your safety harness."

He placed his arm over Jamila again and braced for the landing. They hit the floor of a hanger with a jolt that made his teeth rattle, but he didn't move.

He stood and pulled Jamila to her feet. He leaned down to pick her up and she put her hand on his shoulder.

"I'm all right. I don't feel any pain. I can walk. We need to go back through the window so we don't run into anyone. Luckily, at this time of night, no one is working on the grounds."

He nodded. "Okay, but if you feel faint or your leg hurts tell me and I'll pick you up."

"No problem."

He took her arm anyway and she rolled her eyes. He didn't want her to fall before he could catch her. It was better to lead her by the arm. They made their way slowly around the house as Jamila glanced around like she'd never seen the place before. In spite of her proclamation of feeling more focused, her gaze wandered in odd directions, her eyes vacant.

They reached her window, and he climbed through first and lifted her over before walking her to bed. "Lie right here. Don't move. I need to tell your father that we've arrived so he doesn't come looking for us. If he hasn't already. And I need to get medical supplies."

"Okay, I'm kind of tired and dizzy, so staying here is not a problem."

Of that, he had no doubt.

Chapter Five

He'd saved her life. If he hadn't been there, she would have been killed. She hadn't even realized a grenade had hit the ground until the blast shook the earth. He was right, she didn't know how much danger she was in. She and her father always had threats against their lives. But no one had ever tried that hard to kill her. He'd saved her and been injured in the process. How bad was it? When she'd looked, she couldn't really tell where he'd been hit. Her eyesight was too blurred for that. She thought she'd seen a lot of blood. Would he be okay?

The door hissed faintly as it slid open and the large, slightly blurred figure of Galen came to stand over her bed.

"How you doing?" His deep voice sent shivers up her spine.

"I'm alright. The pain in my leg is starting to come back."

"Right, well, I've brought the regenerator, so I should be able to fix that. Turn over."

She flipped over onto her stomach and he went to work. The faint hum of the medical instrument was the only sound that filled the room.

"You were right to demand I stay home. I should have listened to you. I almost got you killed."

He rubbed his hand over her back. "No, you were doing a good thing. But I wish I'd known what you were doing—we could have come up with a plan that was a little less dangerous. Like, I retrieve the food, and you hover over the city in the shuttle. That sounds much better to me."

"I couldn't tell you what I was doing. I didn't know if you would turn me in."

He clucked his tongue at her. "Come now, Jamila. You know what I am."

"A slave."

He snorted. "Yes, as well as other things. I would never turn someone over who was helping people."

"Yes, but they say most cyborgs have been brainwashed. How would I know you weren't loyal to the government?"

He sighed. "You're right. Definitely don't trust every cyborg you meet. Plenty are loyal to the government. If I had been, you would have known as soon as I found out what you were doing. I would have killed you immediately. We aren't really the 'capture and interrogate' types, unless those are our orders."

She shivered. That was an unpleasant thought. She pushed up so she was leaning on her elbows and glanced at him. "You've known cyborgs loyal to the government?"

"I was one, once. We all were. We were freed when a small group managed to break their brainwashing techniques. They started kidnapping us whenever they found us, and deprogrammed us." His hands shook visibly as he maneuvered the regenerator. "It's a very unpleasant process. And most importantly, it's not always effective, so never tell an unknown cyborg anything."

She laughed but even to her ears it didn't sounds pleasant. "Well, I don't expect to meet many more. Unless someone revokes the kill order on them. You really should find a way to escape this place. It's not safe for you. If you fail my father or he decides you aren't needed, he'll hand you over to the government. They'll kill you for sure."

"I won't be as dead as you'd think. We're an expensive piece of equipment. Even though the government says they're killing us, they're actually pretty desperate to have us back. They've lost billions. More."

That didn't make her worry less. "Then you really should leave. Unless you want to go back to working for them."

"Lord no. Talk about hell. Of course, you don't realize it at the time. Its only after you've been deprogrammed that you figure out they've stolen everything you were. Right down to your soul."

He placed the medical instrument on the bed. "All done." He ran his hand up the back of her thigh until it came to the curve of her butt and then back down again. Little goose bumps followed in the wake of his palm. "Good as new. Why don't you get in the shower and clean up. You're bloody and dirty."

"Right." She pushed herself to sitting and dizziness swamped her. "Wow. I don't think I'm capable of bathing right now. Maybe later." She lay back down and he pulled her back up.

"No, no. I need you clean, and I need to get rid of the evidence of this evening's exciting little adventure, even if I have to shower with you."

She giggled. "Well, that does sound intriguing. Don't think I haven't noticed how very lovely you look shirtless."

And she certainly had. No one was that ripped. It didn't happen. At least no one she'd been around. Eight pack of abs and incredibly defined, broad shoulders, which she'd always found gorgeous on a man. Yep, none of the noblemen her father had set her up with were built like that.

He grinned. "Well, that's always nice to hear from a lady, but the point is to get clean. I need the shower too."

"Hmm…how about giving me that orgasm we were discussing on the ship?"

Good lord. Why had she said that? She couldn't have him. Even though he'd saved her life, he was still dangerous. Being gorgeous didn't change the fact he could cause hull damage to a ship by kicking it. Or that he could probably bend steel. Or that his brain could hack computer systems. Dangerous. Period.

He pulled Jamila to her feet and the world spun. So much for those drugs wearing off. Apparently, they were just getting started.

"This is a bad idea, Galen."

"Don't worry, I won't look."

She snorted. "Since you're supposed to help bathe me, explain how that will work."

"Okay, so I will look, but I'll be strictly professional about it." His voice had dropped into a deep, sensual purr that gave her goose bumps, and his hands were roaming over her back. Yeah, he was going to be professional.

"Why don't I believe that?"

"Because you're hot, and men jump into your bed at regular intervals."

She groaned. Clearly he'd heard too many rumors. Okay, she was no blushing virgin, but she got more action in the media than she ever got in real life.

"Half that shit they say about me is a lie. And even if it weren't, my father has been keeping damned close tabs on me for the last year."

"So you need to get off. I think I can arrange that."

"That's not—"

"Shh. Chill."

She sighed. This was a bad plan. If her father ever suspected, he'd turn Galen over so fast his head would spin. Though she got the feeling telling Galen that wouldn't stop him. He walked her into the bathroom and turned on the water before lifting her onto the counter. He slowly undid the clasps on the flight suit she was wearing all the way to the crotch. He parted the material, baring her breasts.

He sucked in a breath. "You are so tempting. If you weren't hopped up on painkillers, I would take you right here."

He pressed his lips to hers, his tongue plundering her mouth in an imitation of what his body would do to hers if only she could let him. He ran his thumb across her hardening nipple and a little thrill shot straight to her clit.

She broke the kiss as she slid off the counter. She grabbed his hips to steady herself before peeling the tight suit off her body.

"Hmm…the view gets lovelier by the second."

She smiled. "Well, I'd like my view to keep improving too."

He shook his head before his hands went to the buttons of his pants. He released them slowly, watching her reaction as he revealed the dark thatch of hair at the base of his cock. He pushed the pants slowly over his hips until it sprang free. His dick was long, thick, and partially aroused, swelling quickly under her gaze.

She stepped close enough that her nipples brushed his chest and wrapped her hand around his shaft. He let his breath out slowly as she cupped his balls. "The view gets lovelier by the second."

He chuckled and raked his teeth gently over her neck. "As much as I'm enjoying this," he hissed as she gave his cock a leisurely stroke, "the goal really was to shower, and I can't do this right now. Not while you're…"

She squeezed him gently. "While I'm what?"

"Sorry, I lost my train of thought."

She laughed. "Glad I have some power over you."

"Oh, I'd give you all the power if you keep doing that."

"Well, I must say I like the sound of that." But she doubted it was true—he was too aggressive to give up any power. Her pussy was getting soaked. She wanted him in her. She didn't give a damn about the consequences right now.

He laughed and grasped her wrist. She let go of his shaft and he pulled her under the water.

"Enough of that. I do believe it's my turn."

He pressed her against the wall. "You might want to hold onto that bar." He pointed to the hand hold to her left before dropping to his knees in front of her. He lifted her leg and placed it over his shoulder.

"You smell good. Like you're very turned on." He ran his finger around her clit, and down to circle her sex before he dipped his thick finger inside. "Hmm…perfect. Tight and hot and so wet for me." He pumped his finger in and out of her vagina while he rubbed her bud with his thumb.

She gasped and rocked her hips against his hand as he stared at her.

"You're gorgeous when you move like that. Someday I'll have you under me, I swear it."

God, let that day be today. Now. As she approached the edge of orgasm, he removed his hand. Before she could even whimper in protest, he shoved his mouth against her aching clit; his tongue rasped over her with hunger and urgency. He thrust two of his fingers back into her vagina, hard. Sparks of pure pleasure shot up her spine as her pussy clamped down on his invading fingers and she rocked herself against his tongue.

For several seconds he stayed with his head pressed against her inner thigh, while the water rained down on them. His breathing was fast and harsh. He pulled back and dropped her leg. "Go. You need to go in the other room."

"But why? Let me touch you. Let me taste you."

He stood and backed away. "No, go lie down. I shouldn't have gone this far with you. It was wrong. You're out of it, and if you touch me now, I'm not sure what I'll do."

"Everything I want." She took a step toward him and he clasped her shoulders.

"Go get in bed. Now."

She frowned at him, but quickly left the room. Did he really not want to take advantage of her because she was loopy or was it something else? She had enough control to make this decision. He must know that. But he'd made her leave anyway. She glanced over her shoulder. His back was to her, his arms braced on the stall wall. His head was down. Was he ashamed of what they'd done? He didn't want her. In his mind she was a spoiled princess. Not someone he wanted to be with. But she'd hoped even if he didn't want her in the long term, he would want her now. Long term wasn't an option for them.

He stepped back from the wall and grasped his cock in his hand. He stoked it slowly as she watched. Did he sense her eyes on him? His speed built as he tossed his head back, biting his lip. His harsh roar filled the bathroom, echoing off the walls. If she hadn't seen him, she still would have known what he had done. White ropes of cum shot onto the floor of the shower, and coated his hand before rinsing down the drain.

His eyes opened and his heated gaze locked with hers. She spun around and sprinted for her bed. Even after what he'd done to her, it was still embarrassing to get caught watching him jerk off. She flopped onto her stomach in bed, facing her head away from him.

Would he really rather handle himself than be with her? Did she disgust him that much? He was beautiful when he came. She wanted to see it up close. But apparently he didn't want her to.

She sensed, more than heard him as he entered the room, his stare like a physical touch. "Surely you've watched a man masturbate before. You're acting very shy about it."

"No, I haven't. It's something well brought up gentleman deny doing."

He snorted. "I'm sure they do."

"Galen, why did you—"

He grabbed her shoulder and flipped her over. "Believe me, Jamila. I want you. Never doubt that. But I can't have you now, for the reason I've said. And others. I'm a slave, and if anyone found out we were sleeping together, you'd be ostracized and I'd be killed. And there are other things. Things that I can't tell you yet. Someday I intend to have you, but not now."

She sighed. "Whatever. Let me fix your wound. Sit."

He dropped obediently at the foot of her bed, and she reached for the regenerator on the bedside table. She flipped it on and put it to his shoulder wound. It was already scabbed over. It seemed days old rather than hours. "Jeez, whatever super vitamin you're taking, I want some."

He smiled. "Believe me, it's more of a curse than anything."

She could believe it. The government was hunting his kind, and according to him, they'd stolen everything from him.

The regenerator quickly said that healing was complete. She ran her hands over his smooth skin. "That should be it."

"Actually, you need to get the exit wound in the back."

He faced away from her and her gaze fell to it. She lifted the regenerator again. "Wow, the original wound must have been bad."

"Not enough to take me out."

She rolled her eyes. How macho of him. "Clearly. Well, you're all set, even if it wasn't necessary."

He chuckled. "Thank you, but you should probably stop running your palms over my back."

She jerked her hands away. "Right."

He turned around, tangled his hands in her hair, and pulled her into a short, scorching kiss. He pulled away and rested his forehead against hers.

"I shouldn't have done that."

She pulled away with a grumble. "Why?"

He grabbed her hand and wrapped it around his stiffening cock.

She snickered. "Oops."

He stood, and she let her hand slip down his dick.

"Goodnight, Jamila."

She leaned back on the bed and ran her hands lightly over her breasts and down her thighs. "You sure you don't want me to take care of that?"

He closed his eyes as if praying for patience, or restraint. "God yes, but its late. Get some sleep. Your father said you have a suitor tomorrow."

"Fuck. Yeah. Like I'm going to sleep now."

Chapter Six

Jamila tried to hide her smirk as she watched Galen over the shoulder of this jerk. He was making faces at him, trying to cheer her up. She'd been in a foul mood all morning. Something directly related to the skinny, whining man sitting across from her. He'd arrived early. Six in the morning. That was quite enough to make her hate him, when her father had roused her and Galen only three hours after they'd gotten to bed. Galen was a much better sport than her. He'd called her spoiled again, but ruffled her hair as he said it.

"You're not used to getting up early. I'm used to being roused with a beating. Your father calling me over an intercom, albeit a loud one, is a much better wake up call, trust me."

But he'd quickly lost his patience as well when they'd gone to breakfast to find her father and William Reginald Barry the Third debating the finer points of the upcoming elections. She'd almost fallen asleep at the table, Galen standing silently at her back.

Now they'd been left alone with the horrible William. She restrained another sigh. She'd spent her morning sighing, and Mr. Pompous Ass still wouldn't shut his trap. He'd also insulted her several times, saying basically that women weren't equal to men or as smart as them.

When she'd expressed her opinion on keeping the genetically engineered locked away in Haven districts, his response had been, "You have no sense, dear. You don't know what you're talking about. I've met these people. They're dangerous."

Only Galen's hand on her shoulder had stopped her from popping him in the mouth. Just when she'd seriously considered jumping off the SkyTemple from the balcony in the breakfast nook, Galen had changed positions, and started entertaining her.

"What do you find so funny now, Miss Clearborne?"

She coughed and straightened in her seat. "Oh, nothing. I was only smiling at you. You're very witty and charming."

She could almost gag on the lie as she forced it out. Billy-boy beamed at her, revealing rows of solid gold teeth, something popular among the gentry, and she tried not to flinch.

"I'm pleased you find me charming, my dear." He grabbed her hand in his clammy palm and kissed her knuckles, leaving imprints of blue lip tar on her. She didn't jerk it back, but oh how she wanted to. She'd never understand the latest trend in blue lipstick. Particularly the shade he was wearing. It was like a dead blue grey. Like he'd died of hypothermia. If only.

She glanced at Galen, only to find he wasn't staring at her anymore. His gaze was fixed on the news feed screen mounted above the far end of the table. His jaw clenched and his grip tightened on his wrist, causing the muscles in his arms to stand out. What had him so riled up? His gaze shot to hers, and he jerked his head toward the screen. She nodded slightly and turned her full attention to it.

Houses were on fire, their ancient wooden flames not able to hold up. The camera panned over the whole region. A whole town was completely demolished.

The little caption finally gave the location. Haven District, Larus. The bottom dropped out of her stomach and she stood so quickly her chair crashed to the floor.

"Volume up!" she shouted as she stumbled toward the end of the table.

"...twenty thousand dead. And an estimated one hundred thousand injured or missing. Look at that devastation! The government's bombs ripped this area apart this morning just after four in the morning."

Her insides churned at the excited tone in the announcer's voice. She tried to halt her shaking. It would do no good to show William what this news was doing to her.

And then the asshole opened his mouth. "Good riddance, I say. The government said they did it because the people were breaking the law and going into the districts around them, but I say they have every right to kill them all. They're nothing but trouble. Riffraff who want to take over the world and kill people like us. I hope they catch the people that were aiding them."

"What?" Bile rose in her throat as she tried to wrestle her panic. They knew someone was helping them? She had to assume they didn't know who yet, or agents would be knocking at her door. Well, not knocking. Kicking down.

"Yes, they think some people were smuggling them food, medical supplies, and weapons." Weapons? She'd never run weapons. Maybe they would be catching someone else instead of her. Galen jerked and he glared at her, the muscle in his jaw twitching.

William picked a piece of lint off his cuff. "They should bomb all those places. Sometimes the government is much too humane."

The camera panned the house where the children were. There was nothing left. The place had been leveled. God, where were they? Was anyone alive? She couldn't believe this.

She turned on William, and strode toward him.

"Jamila, no." Galen's harshly barked order didn't even make her pause.

She slammed her fist into William's face and he crashed to the ground. "Get out of my house. Anyone who would revel in the deaths of so many people doesn't deserve to lick my shoes. I will never marry you, you piece of shit."

She aimed a kick to his ribs when she was lifted off her feet. Galen hauled her against his body and quickly carried her out of the room. She drummed her heels against his shins, trying to get him to let her go.

"Come on, dammit. Let me kick him a few times. Put me down."

He shoved her in her room and she stumbled to her knees. She ground her teeth as pain shot up her thighs. He quietly shut the door behind him, as he rubbed the bridge of his nose.

"I hate that man. You should have let me beat him a little more."

He froze, and slowly lowered his hand. "Do you know what you've done?"

Her eyes filled with tears. Why did he have to remind her? She'd gotten those people killed. She knew that. If she hadn't been trading with them they wouldn't have died. "It's my fault. I killed them as thoroughly as if I'd shot them. Do you have to bring that up now? I know I'm as guilty as the government."

He growled, leaned over, and plucked her off the ground by her arms. He shook her. "You don't know what you've done. You've revealed yourself, and you didn't even hesitate to do it." He pointed back toward the sitting room. "Those actions in there? Punching him? You're obvious reaction to those deaths? He witnessed that. He knows you're a damned sympathizer now. What if he suspects what you've done? Dammit, Jamila, why didn't you think?"

She shook her head. This was why he was upset? She didn't give a damn. So she'd revealed herself. It was worth it to get a shot at his smug face. "He won't turn me in. He doesn't know I was smuggling medical supplies and food to those people. He's probably stupid enough not to even suspe—"

He shook her. "Goddammit! Don't be so blind. He might act like a damned moron, but he is an educated man. If you think he doesn't suspect you now then you're as stupid as he claims."

He shoved her down on the bed, and paced away from her. He rounded on her again, and took a deep breath, seeming to reconsider his words. He walked away again, and when he turned he kept his distance.

"Were you giving them weapons, Jamila? I need the truth. You're in horrible danger if you did. You're the person they will hunt down first. I'd bet you anything the government already knows about your involvement. If you were running arms, you'll be killed. If you weren't, they might not even come after you. Tell me the truth."

She shook her head frantically. "I never gave them weapons. I swear. Food and medicine. I was working with an orphanage, for God's sake."

He nodded. "That might save you too. I assume they went in because they heard that the underground was receiving guns. They might not even find out about you until they torture Alice, Darion, or one of the children."

"Torture? You don't think they're dead? We have to help them if they're being tortured."

His gaze softened. "There's nothing we can do, sweeting. They're probably on their way to a core planet to be more thoroughly interrogated. Even if they're still here, if we tried to rescue them, we'd end up dead."

Pain radiated from her chest, making it hard to breathe. She rubbed her breastbone, but couldn't seem to get a full breath. They were dead, or being tortured. What if she had gotten them killed? Had they been spotted crossing the wall last night? She buried her head in her hands.

She felt the bed dip under Galen's weight. He pulled her into his arms and hugged her tight. He didn't say a word, thankfully. She didn't need any dull platitudes about how everything would be okay, and it wasn't her fault. She needed him to hold her for a while.

• • •

Galen laid Jamila's sleeping form on the bed and stood. He crossed to his room and shut the door. He couldn't wait now. He had to act. This wasn't something he'd expected. He might not even be able to get what he wanted now, due to her criminal actions. He had to hope she was still worth something to her father. He hacked his slave collar and shackles and they hit the throw rug with a dull thud. They'd been blocking the transmitter under the skin on the back of his hand. The slaver had missed it, as they'd expected, along with the communications device under the flesh of his palm.

He opened his hand and whispered. "Change of plan. Come get me. Now!"

Chapter Seven

A deafening boom shook the house. Jamila hit the ground on her backside in a tangle of silk sheets and barely kept her head from striking the floor. What the fuck was that? She rubbed her bruised butt as she sat up.

It happened again and SkyTemple tilted violently to the left. Her bookshelf whined as it rocked. The house settled again.

"Galen?" He didn't answer and that was as frightening as anything else.

She scrambled to get away from the bed. If the bookshelf fell, all her ancient leather bound books would crush it. She pushed herself to her feet, got stuck in the stupid silk sheets and hit the marble floor again. She needed to get into the hall where there was no furniture. In ships all the furniture was bolted down, but in Temples, after the initial launch they barely moved at all, and if they did they did it slowly.

"Galen? I need some help." Where was he? He should have been in here. He'd been here when she'd fallen asleep.

Then she got help, but not the kind she wanted. The temple pitched again. The silk sheets, and her along with them, slid and hit the wall. Pain exploded in her head and she gasped for air trying to regain her balance. She touched her forehead and came away with blood.

The bookshelf crashed onto the bed and the whole mess slid a foot toward her with a groan before the house started to level out.

She kicked free of the sheets and crawled into the hallway, using the doorway to pull herself up. She had to get the servants and find a shuttle to get off this thing. She turned and crashed right into Galen.

"Where have you been? I've been calling for you. I was frightened. The stabilizers must be malfunctioning."

He brushed his hand over the cut on her forehead and she flinched. "Dammit. I thought you'd at least be safe in your rooms. I can't leave you alone for a second. Sorry about that. I had to take care of some things."

"What's happening?"

"The stabilizers are fine. Your SkyTemple is taking fire."

She gaped at him, not believing it. No one had ever tried to shoot down one of them before. "What? Why?"

"Because your father is a high ranking government official with numerous enemies, that's why."

"But he's left. Elections are taking place and the Senate has one last meeting. Everyone knows where he is."

"Yeah, well I get the feeling they aren't here for your daddy, sweetheart." Sarcasm and contempt colored his words. He'd never directed that much loathing toward her, even when he'd first been bought.

His hand tightened painfully on her arm and she flinched and smacked his fingers. "What's wrong with you? You're hurting me. Besides, what you're suggesting is ludicrous. I'm of use to no one. My father won't bow to terrorists."

His grip loosened, but he didn't let go. "I'm not necessarily talking about you, though you would be useful, despite what you think."

She frowned. Why would they be attacking if not to hurt her or her father? He pulled her down the hallway. They'd made it a few feet before she realized they weren't heading toward the shuttles and she pulled him to a stop.

"Galen, the shuttles are back this way."

"Not the one I'm going for."

Another blast rocked the house and she almost tumbled to the ground. Galen kept his footing with minimal effort. As he helped her regain her balance, her eyes narrowed on his bare wrists.

She tried to yank her arm from his grip. "Where are your servant's bands?" If they were gone it meant he'd escaped them. She shivered. She was in danger if he had.

"Don't worry about them. I need to get you out of here. We might be killed if we stay."

She needed to stall him. She couldn't place this uneasy feeling, but she didn't want to go with him anymore. "But what about everyone else?"

"They'll be alright."

She tugged on him to get him to stop pulling her. "The servants might be killed. And I want to know why you don't have your slave's bands on? How did you get them off?"

He paused long enough to toss her over his shoulder.

"Galen, dammit! What are you doing? Put me down."

"Nope. It's my job to see that you're safe, and I'm going to damned well do it, so you lie there and be silent."

Panic froze her as her brain tried to work out what was happening. If he didn't have his servant's bands, he was at least twice as strong as he'd been with them on. And there was no way to incapacitate him remotely if they were gone. It couldn't be good that he was without them. But he'd saved her life before. Could she really doubt him? He was being rude, but in a dangerous situation that seemed to be his way…but why did she get the gut feeling that he was lying to her face?

"Galen, please stop—" Her protest died mid-sentence as they passed over a form crumpled in the hallway. One of the guards. They passed by so quickly that she couldn't tell if the man was dead or not. Galen hadn't even paused. Why? Did he know the man's fate?

Galen can probably read his life signs without touching him.

Or had he killed him?

"Please tell me what's going on. You're frightening me."

He grunted, and kept walking. She slammed her fists into his back, but she couldn't cause him pain. She knew that. She could pummel his back until she broke her hands and he wouldn't even flinch.

The lights flickered and then they were plunged into darkness. It didn't stop him though. He walked like he could see perfectly in front of him. Like he had last night in the alley. She couldn't do anything. She hung there useless over his shoulder.

There was one thing she could do. She took a deep breath, opened her mouth, and screamed for all she was worth.

"Dammit, woman. Are you trying to bust my eardrums? You can scream all you want but I'll kill anyone who comes after us. I think I managed to take out most of the guards here anyway."

Dead? "Did you kill all of them?"

He sighed. "Some. When they realized what was happening and who was attacking, I was their first target."

Who was attacking? More cyborgs? It must be. Nothing else would make the security team attack Galen.

He kicked open the door that led out to the patio and set her down. Light blinded her. It was a beautiful, sunny day for the middle of winter but the cold still permeated her clothes. There was hum of a ship behind her. She whirled around and got a look at what was there.

It was a massive shuttle, with guns mounted haphazardly on it. It clearly hadn't originally been fashioned with them. It was big enough to fit twenty passengers comfortably. More if they were traveling a short distance. Ten men were lined up outside of it, and one stood in front of the rest.

"Shit, Galen, don't scare us like that. We were about to go in after you." The man in front stepped forward, and grasped his hand. "Good to see you. A month is too long."

Galen snorted. "Yeah, and I've only been here for two days. Being in the slave trade isn't all it's cracked up to be."

The man leaned around Galen to get a better view of her. "But I see you got the prize. Which wasn't guaranteed."

"Yep."

Got the prize? Like hell. She turned and bolted for the doors. She'd show him. He shouldn't have released her if he expected to keep her. She slid in through the patio doors, right into the arms of another tall cyborg. She kicked his shin as hard as she could and cursed as pain shot up her foot. She was an idiot. She couldn't hurt one of these men in shoes, let alone without them. All she'd get was broken toes for her trouble.

"Now, now, none of that. I believe you're supposed to stay with the group."

He grabbed her upper arm and hauled her back into the yard. "Galen, I think you misplaced someone."

He shoved her toward Galen hard. She almost hit the ground when he saved her from the fall, wrapping his arms around her and pinning her to his chest.

"Fuck, Torin. Be careful. You don't need to hurt her."

"She tried to run, thanks to your poor supervision. Besides, I'm used to dealing with our women. One of them wouldn't have stumbled like that."

Galen stepped away from her but kept his hold on her arm. "Which is why no one touches her but me, and if you have to, use a light hand. You could easily kill her. And as for running, what do you really expect? It's not like she can get away."

"It could have taken us hours to search this place if you'd let her go."

He smiled. "I could have caught her. She can't outrun me. And I knew your team was coming through there anyway. Now let's load up and get the hell out of here. It's only a matter of time before the Ops show up, and since they're our people, we'd be badly outmatched in that little death trap of a shuttle you've fixed up."

He skimmed his hand down her arm and laced his fingers with hers, tightening his grip when she tried to pull away.

"Where are you taking me? Let go!"

He shook his head and forced her to walk toward the ship. "I'm taking you to the rest of our people for a few weeks. See, the senate is trying to pass a law that would give the government the funds and manpower to hunt down and kill all of us. Your father can make a big difference in that. He has a considerable amount of power in a room where many of the senators are on the fence about the issue, even if their only reason is that we're expensive. Your father isn't. He wants us killed. He's the swing vote. If he switches to our side, many will follow."

"Kidnapping me won't help your case. He's not going to change his decision because you've taken me."

"Then you'll die. I suspect he cares enough about you to save you from that."

They walked up the ramp of the shuttle in silence and he shoved her into a chair. He belted her in.

"Computer, lock this seat."

There was a click as it locked and dread shot through Jamila's veins like ice water. "This is a prisoner transport chair."

He nodded. "Ripped from the latest and greatest government vessel."

"You don't have to lock me up. What can I possibly do?"

He smiled. "Plenty. I'm quickly learning not to underestimate you."

He stood and faced the man who'd caught her, Torin. "Did you do that other thing I asked of you?"

He nodded and glanced at her. "Yeah, but I don't get why you wanted it done. It's a dangerous mission to get a handful of people."

"They're important. And they might spill and make this whole operation useless."

She hung her head and stopped listening to them. She'd trusted him, and he'd betrayed her. It was her own damn fault. She should have known better. He was a freaking cyborg, with his own agenda. But she'd thought he at least cared for her a little. She was wrong. He was going to kill her if her father didn't give in to his demands. And Cyrus wouldn't. If anything, this little act would make him lose it and hunt them all down. Of course, she'd be long dead before he could exterminate them.

Galen sat in the chair next to her. "Get us out of here before police show."

The door closed as the ship launched immediately. They must have left it heated while searching for Galen, so they didn't have to spare time warming up. A sound plan. Galen kept glancing at her. After a minute of having him watch her, she couldn't take it anymore. He was trying to make her crazy.

"Why do you keep staring at me? Leave me alone. Why don't you go sit somewhere else? I can't stand having you near me."

"I have to watch you. It's my job to get you from here to the station. Period."

"I can't exactly escape if I'm fucking bolted in the seat, so I think you can leave. What, are you waiting for me to burst into tears? Scream at you? What?"

"I don't know what I'm waiting for. I definitely don't want you to have a breakdown, but I'm fearing you will."

Oh, she was definitely on the verge of a breakdown, but she couldn't tell him that. She wouldn't show weakness to this man. Never again. He'd gotten her trust, and taken advantage of it.

"Where are you taking me?"

"An outpost on the edge of this system."

"What's out there?" She knew one thing that was out there. Aliens. Hostile aliens. There were no humans out that far. Since serious space exploration had begun, they'd come into contact with very few alien races. Half were too underdeveloped to interact with. However, they'd made contact with two other races. One thought humans were too violent, and had severed all contact due to several confrontations, and monitoring Earth's news stations. The other race was purely predatory. They wanted resources, slave labor, planets to colonize and blood. She shuddered and hoped that last rumor wasn't true. Humans had a tentative treaty with them, when they had proved to be too much of a pain in the ass to eliminate completely. They'd settled for trade. But more than one trade mission had been massacred. Or taken. No one was really sure but it seemed humans offended other races no matter where they went. The Corabin found almost every gesture and word to be an offense.

"We have a small space station out there. A long term living space left over from when human space travel was less developed."

Good lord. They were going to die. Those things were rickety and most had been scrapped years ago when miners had discovered better materials to make the stations out of. Pre-advanced space travel? They were lucky life support hadn't failed, or an airlock hadn't vented them all out into space.

She snorted. "So you do plan to kill me? I thought you were waiting until my father said no to your demands?"

He rolled his eyes. "We've fixed it, and it's been in good working order for years. And most importantly the government doesn't monitor what they believe is trash."

"And what rickety ship are we taking there?"

He grinned. "Oh, it's not rickety at all. I can't wait to show you. It's my baby."

Her curiosity got the better of her. "What ship is it? Did you steal it?"

"Sure did. All by my lonesome. And when you see it, you'll understand why I am so very proud of myself."

She eyed him. "Tell me now."

"Nope. Won't do it."

They sat in silence for a while. She might be curious about the ship he'd stolen, but she was still pissed, and not prepared to forgive him. Ever. How did he engage her in conversation so quickly? She would ignore him from now on. She nodded to herself, cementing her resolve.

The proximity alarm in the ship went off and she jolted. Either they were coming up to something, or they were being shot at. The jumper rocked from an impact.

"We're taking fire."

A second blast pitched the small spacecraft to the left.

"Shit." Galen unstrapped himself and stood. "I knew they'd come after you. Dammit." He dashed for the pilot's compartment, and leaned over Torin's shoulder.

"Any identification yet?"

Torin nodded. "Government Police five-five-six. They've—"

The speakers crackled before the message came over the intercom. "Unknown vessel, kill your engines and prepare to be boarded or you will be fired upon."

"Requested that we stop."

Galen snorted. "Yeah, I got that. Options?"

"We're faster and more maneuverable. If we full burn, we can make it back to the Mother. But—"

"There's a forty-one point seven percent chance we'll explode."

The pilot titled his head back and forth. "Well, with the upgrades it's more like thirty five. We could also open fire. But—"

"Their guns are bigger, better, and they have more than we do."

"We must be soul mates. Can't you let me finish a sentence?"

"Nope, it's easier this way." Galen hit a yellow button on the dash. "Government vessel, I have a senator's daughter onboard. If you don't turn around, I'll kill her."

"We don't negotiate with terrorists."

Jamila dropped her head back on the neck rest. She was a dead woman.

Galen sighed. "Great. Bring us around and blow out their engines. You'll only get one shot at it, so make it count. Then get us out of here. Full burn."

"Gotcha."

Jamila rattled her harness. She knew she couldn't pull it off, but that didn't stop her from trying. "Galen, this is crazy. Let me go in a life pod. They'll be too busy picking me up to go after you if you go fast. You're going to get us all killed."

He glared at her. "I think I know what I'm doing a little better than you."

"Let me go."

Torin glanced over his shoulder at her. "You don't get it, we need you. We can't let you go. If we die, then we die. But I get the feeling they won't destroy us with you here, no matter what they say. Senators are very powerful men. Even if we get away, they'll likely look for other ways to get you back. It would mean riches and rank for anyone who managed."

"I'm really not worth that much. If you think taking me will convince my father to do anything for you, you're wrong."

Galen held up his hand. "Jamila, hush. You can't talk me out of this."

She bit her lip to keep from screaming at him. They were going to get her killed before they even had a chance to murder her themselves. This was proof that he was one of the crazy genetically engineered people. He was unreasonable. She didn't want to go to their space station. They were probably all as crazy as Galen.

The ship spun around so fast that even the inertial dampeners didn't reduce the feeling of nausea that swamped her. She watched the government ship as they accelerated dangerously toward it. She clenched her fists. When she was sure they'd hit it, the jumper dipped and flew under the police vessel just in time. They fired, and veered away.

"Punch it!"

The sudden momentum shoved her back against the chair. The air forced from her lungs as they hit full burn. She struggled to breathe as pressure threatened to crush her chest. As suddenly as it came, it was gone, as they reached a constant speed.

Galen slapped Torin on the shoulder. "Nicely done."

"Thank you, I'll take a fucking bow later."

Galen walked back to his seat and collapsed into it with a grin on his face. "I was a little worried there. I didn't think they would be able to respond so fast to your abduction."

"Bully for you. Are you actually happy about this? You were almost caught and you're smiling."

He shrugged. "Cyborgs were built for battle. It's exciting. Cheer up, Jamila. We made it out alive and soon we'll be on the ship. You'll get to roam, within reason. And you'll get some food. I'm sure you're starving."

"Like I'd eat anything you'd give me."

He rolled his eyes. "I'm not going to poison you. I need you."

"Until you don't need me, and then you'll kill me."

He glanced away from her. "It won't come to that."

"So you say. Forgive me, but I find it hard to believe someone who's betrayed me. It's a fault of mine."

He sighed, closed his eyes, and settled back in his seat.

She shook her head, and looked away from him. The other cyborgs watched her. Why? The gaze of one flickered to Galen, and his eyes narrowed. What was he thinking? Probably that she and Galen were closer than they were. At least she'd never actually slept with him. Though, she'd done everything but. Shame swept through her. She was an idiot. She knew she wasn't some uptight prude, but this? Letting a cyborg slave go down on her, and then being screwed over by him? Things couldn't get much worse. She closed her eyes and tried to think about something else.

Chapter Eight

She jumped as the click of her harness being released woke her. Her head pounded.

"Whoa, easy there. You're safe."

She blinked up at Galen and smiled tightly, trying to ignore the pain in her head so she didn't take it out on him. His eyes widened. She glanced around and realized why he was shocked. She was surrounded by cyborgs, and on her way to some space station in a dangerous part of the solar system. She should be cursing this man.

She pushed herself to her feet and swayed as a spike of pain jabbed her right behind the eyes.

Galen grabbed her elbow. "Are you okay?"

She shook her head. "I'll be fine. I have a migraine."

He frowned at her. "That doesn't sound fine. Don't worry, we'll get you food and water and a painkiller.

"Food and a painkiller sound lovely."

He shook his head. "Are you having any dizziness?"

She sighed. "No."

"Good. Tell me if you do. We'll have to go to medical."

He led her off the jumper before the other cyborgs finished collecting their gear. They stepped into a huge cargo bay.

She stared at the cyborgs bustling around multiple smaller ships as they unloaded crates and made repairs. "I've never seen a ship this big unless it was a government ship.

He chuckled. "And who do you think we steal ships from? It would hardly be sporting to take them from plain old citizens when it's the government we want to take down."

She gaped at him. "Take down? You're an anarchist then?"

"No. We don't like who's in power now. They're corrupt. They made us like this. They continue to turn people into cyborgs, and by doing so they're destroying lives. You don't know how many people they've ripped from their families. Sometimes their families were even murdered. Other times they were left to starve without husbands to support them. Most women hold factory jobs or are whores. They take people from the poorest regions of society because we have no claim to fight back. They left my family to die."

He'd started out composed, but by the end of his speech he'd grown tense, his voice rising. Not enough to shout, but he certainly hadn't been quiet. He rolled his shoulders and took a deep breath.

"Sorry, I didn't mean to rant. But the bottom line is they're taking advantage of their power. They need to be stopped before they kill more people."

"So you'd send everything into chaos because you dislike the government."

He smirked. "Not chaos. We have a plan."

"You know, you sound like those crazy genetically engineered armies. The ones that were messed up. They wanted to take over the government too. Look where it got them. Look where it got you."

"We don't plan to run the government. We have people loyal to us among the senate. Not everyone wants us killed."

She rolled her eyes. "Now that shocks me."

He gazed deep into her eyes like he was trying to read her, while revealing nothing of himself. "You don't really want me dead. Or any of us. You think it's as much of an injustice as keeping the genetically engineered in ghettos."

"This is different. You're ten times more of a threat than the Gens are. You have a brain rivaling a computer. You have reinforced skeletons. I'm sure you know your fair amount of government secrets, and you're stealing their ships."

"You still don't think we should be stuck out here, rotting in space under threat of death if we're caught. Admit it."

She glared at him. She wasn't going to say it. He was right of course. No one deserved this. But when they behaved as they were, who could blame the government for wanting them contained.

"Fine. Don't say it, but I know you believe it. Your actions prove it." He turned and stormed away from her. "Keep up, or I'll assign you another guard and be done with you."

She'd pissed him off. She couldn't help it. She refused to insinuate that it was a good idea to overthrow the government. She didn't agree with that. It would get many more people killed. He said they had friends in high places, but there was no way to ensure that their favored leader would get the position, and despite their belief that he or she was on their side, he probably couldn't even get laws passed to save them.

She looked around the ship as she followed closely behind him. It all seemed so familiar. Like she'd been here before, or …

She stopped and her jaw dropped as she stared at the walls around her. There was only one ship this size that had been stolen in the past decade. "This is Vengeance!"

Galen turned around and smirked at her. "Yes, yes it is."

She gaped at him. "But how? It was state of the art. Guarded by half the military and then there was its crew. How did you do this?"

"Well, with a whole strike force it would have been impossible, but with one man? It was easy to slip in unnoticed. I hid in the repair tunnels, and started wreaking havoc on their systems. It took me days, but I found environmental controls and alerted them that the ship was going to be flooded with neurotoxic gases. Everyone made a mad dash for the exits, when really all I did was hold my breath and slowly vent the atmosphere. I can hold my breath for twenty minutes. See, I'm still human. I didn't even break any records. Then I released a life pod of people who didn't quite make it out."

He grinned. "It turned out that stealing it was the easy part. Piloting it with one person? Significantly harder. More than one system tends to require your attention at once, and multitasking can be dangerous while flying a ship alone."

She shook her head. "But you made it."

"That I did. I managed to use autopilot, which while not preferred, was a huge help because I had to maintain the ship's systems and yank out the fucking tracking system in it. It also had a remote self-destruct. I guess they were reluctant to use it though. Now if they do, they'll blow up a chunk of asteroid and send it careening toward the capitol building. It took some math, but I think I got the trajectory right."

"You're big on bragging, aren't you?"

"Pfft. Kiss my ass. I am male, after all. We do our fair share of gloating. I am still unmatched for thefts of government vessels. Though I'm hoping Kyle does better. I don't mind losing my title of Reigning Theft Champion for a new ship."

She couldn't help laughing. "There's a title?"

"Yep, with a trophy."

She rolled her eyes. "Oh, that I have to see."

He leaned over and whispered in her ear. "Well, I'm sure I can arrange that. It's on a shelf above my bed."

She shook her head and stepped away from him. "You know that won't happen. You ruined your chances. I can't ever trust you again."

His gaze turned solemn. "I suspected as much. A shame. You're a beautiful, special woman and I want you. But it will be worth it if we can get what we need. Besides, I don't intend to stop trying to seduce you. Follow me."

He turned and walked away while she glared at his back. Couldn't he just let it go? But it *was* a shame. He was just as incredible to her. She'd thought he was a wonderful person. He had legitimate reasons for what he'd done, but he'd still taken her from home into a dangerous situation. She trailed behind him, and couldn't help but notice the scowls of the other cyborgs as they passed. They didn't like her. It was another tally in the danger column. She couldn't forgive him, no matter what his reasons.

The door in front of them slid open and they stepped inside. It was the mess hall. Several cyborgs were sitting around chatting. A few were women, but there were mostly men. Everyone's eyes shifted to her and the hair on the back of her neck stood on end. Every single gaze held hostility. She edged closer to Galen. No matter what he'd done, he hadn't physically injured her. She felt safer near him.

He stuck his hand out behind him as if he sensed that she needed something to give her strength. She grasped it and he pulled her through the room to sit at an empty table.

"I'm going to get us some food. Sit tight. No one will hurt you, and I'll be right over there."

He pointed to the line across the room.

She nodded. She could sit here for five minutes while he got food. She glanced around at the enraged faces as he strolled away and hoped he came back soon. Instead of glancing at him with apprehension, she closed her eyes and massaged her pounding temples. Nothing helped when she got migraines like this. It was going to hurt until he gave her pain meds to knock her out. Hopefully she could keep food down. It was a problem occasionally, if the agony got too intense.

"Hello, human."

She opened her eyes, and gaped at the Amazon standing over her. Jamila was tall, but this woman would have rivaled Galen. She was ripped too, like a female body builder. Were cyborgs built that way or did they spend time bulking up? She smiled at the woman, and prayed that being polite would help with any hostility. Judging by the woman's deepening frown, it wouldn't.

"Can I help you?"

"You're awfully scrawny for one of our men. A few were wondering if you would survive them taking you."

That had occurred to her too. Galen was always gentle, but if he lost control it wouldn't end well for her.

"Honestly, I don't know, and I don't intend to find out."

"Why? Too good to fuck a cyborg?"

"If you're going to put words in my mouth, I'm going to nap, and you can have this conversation by yourself, okay?"

It sounded rude, even to her ears. Damn the migraine. It made you go for the throat every time, even with people you liked.

When the woman smiled, a little chill went down Jamila's spine. "Well, I'd love to know if you can take one of them. They're rather aggressive in bed, and they don't seem to like you very much." She turned and shouted to the men in a language Jamila didn't understand. They laughed, and some eyed Jamila with obvious lust.

"What did you say to them?"

"Nothing, little human. I'm sure you'll find out."

Her hands flashed out so fast Jamila didn't see them coming before they were tangled in her hair. The woman wrenched her neck back and she couldn't contain the small gasp of pain. "By the way, Galen is mine. I'll make sure you pay if he fucks you."

"Ann! Let her go, now," Galen shouted from across the room. His long legs ate up the distance as he came to her aid.

She met Ann's gaze. "He'll beat you bloody if I tell him you've threatened me. He already knows what you said to the room. I'm guessing it was unkind, dirty, or threatening. Do you really want to wait around for him to make it over here?"

Ann released her, and fear darkened the woman's features. She turned and stalked away. Jamila took a breath in relief and rotated her neck. Ann had pulled it so hard that it would be sore for days. If she could only go back and start today over.

Galen reached her side and thumped two prepackaged meals on the table. He cupped his hand over her neck and massaged gently. "Did she hurt you? What did she say?"

"Yes, she hurt me, but not much. And she threatened me. Said you were her fuck buddy and I should keep my distance."

He snorted. "I'm hardly hers. We had sex before I left for my mission, over a month ago. I can't believe she hasn't found someone else."

"Whatever. You're not mine. Keep her away from me. What did she shout to the room?"

His knuckles cracked as his hands clenched into fists. "That you wanted to be fucked by one of us. That you couldn't wait. Don't worry. I'll have a talk with them after I take you to your room. I won't let any harm come to you."

She was starting to think he couldn't prevent it.

• • •

He watched as she ate. She grimaced with every bite. It wasn't the kind of food she was used to. This was only a little better than what she'd given the orphans in the Haven district. It was for survival, not to invigorate your senses with decadence. He was sorry he couldn't offer her more. Though surely she'd traveled and eaten similar food.

She pushed away her half eaten meal and massaged her temples. This headache worried him. Her little bump on the head shouldn't have caused such a powerful migraine. Cyborgs didn't get headaches. Was something wrong with her? Surely if there was it would have been detected by her doctors and removed. It was time to take her to lie down.

"Are you done?"

"Yes, it tastes horrible."

"Sorry about that; the meals aren't going to get any better either. We're searching for a planet to settle on, but the search for a habitable one is difficult. Until then we have to deal with the rations we steal."

She sighed. "Sorry, I didn't mean to be rude."

He snorted. "I think you have every right to be. It's not a problem. I can handle one crabby, small woman."

She glared at him. "Yeah, until I rack you."

He arched a brow. "I'm pretty sure I could grab you before you managed that."

He stood and held out his hand and helped her up. They quickly exited the dining hall while he glowered at everyone who dared to stare at her. This was one problem he had to deal with. It had taken him quite a bit of restraint not to injure her by accident. If one of these men went near her…he didn't even want to think about what would happen. Especially if someone decided to have sex with her. He knew she wouldn't consent to that and it would probably get her killed. He rubbed his thumb over her knuckles. He loathed putting her in this situation. She'd proved to be a good person, despite her upbringing. She didn't deserve to be threatened by his people.

Ann's reaction puzzled him. The sex between them was casual. No strings. It often was among cyborgs. And yet she acted like she possessed him. He'd have to set her straight. He belonged to no one, and right now, the only person he wanted to fuck was clutching his hand like a lifeline.

He glanced at Jamila. She still trusted him, even though she said she never would again. He was the lesser of evils. Not a compliment, but it wasn't hopeless to try and wiggle his way back into her good graces. Well, if he didn't have to maintain the act that he would kill her if they didn't get what they wanted from her father. If they let her communicate with her father at all, she had to believe her life was in danger. It put an unfortunate kink in his plan to seduce her. Nothing he couldn't get around but he regretted causing her stress.

He arrived at the door to his chambers and it slid open. He pulled her inside and sat her on the bed. "Why don't you shower while I get you a painkiller?"

She nodded and he left, silently locking the door behind him. He couldn't bear watching her get undressed. Not while she was in his room, and would be sleeping in his bed. He shook his head. He was a grown man. He could handle a beautiful woman sleeping next to him. He snorted. No he couldn't.

He turned the corner a few feet from the infirmary and spotted Ann sashaying toward him. "Do you want her, Galen? Don't deny it. I've seen the way you stared at her. Held her hand."

Just what he wanted to do right now; arguing with Ann was annoying at best. "If you know the answer, why ask the question? I want her, but I can't have her, so it's moot. She doesn't want me back." He was positive that wasn't true, but he wasn't about to share that with Ann.

Ann trailed a finger down his shirt. "Why don't you come with me then, and work out your frustrations. We had incredible sex."

It had been alright. She was a little too fake for his tastes. He got her off, but none of her responses were genuine. Not like Jamila. Every time he touched her, he could see exactly what she was feeling. Exactly what he did to her. It was intoxicating.

"No, thank you. I have to keep an eye on her. I don't have time to fuck you. If I don't get back, she may try to escape."

"Then tie her up. You should put her in a holding cell anyway."

"She's not a criminal, Ann. She's not even dangerous. But she is resourceful. By the way, don't ever threaten her again. Stay away from her. She's not a threat to you, and she's a good person who doesn't deserve anything we're doing to her. If you hurt her, I'll make sure you suffer."

She snarled. "She's human. They deserve whatever they get." She turned and stalked off. He ground his teeth. She wasn't going to stop. He was going to have to watch Jamila and keep her far away from Ann. He finished his walk to the infirmary and grabbed a painkiller.

When he made it back to his room, Jamila was face down on the bed in one of his shirts. It rode up, and didn't cover her ass all the way. He bit back a moan as his cock hardened in a rush. Her long legs hung over the edge of the bed, and all he could imagine doing was spreading them and plunging into her wet, warm cunt from behind. *Stop. Her head aches. And she's still angry with you.* No matter how much he repeated that mantra, his libido refused to listen.

"Jamila, are you asleep?" he whispered.

"No. Head hurts too much to sleep."

He adjusted his hard on before walking to her side. "Well I brought you something for that." He lifted her hair and injected her with the medicine he'd brought. "That should help."

He was distracted by the back of her neck. The little peach fuzz stood on end. Was his touch affecting her? Could she feel the heat of his gaze on her body? He slid a hand through her hair and massaged her scalp.

"Hmm…that feels nice."

Yes, it did. Her hair was soft and shiny. What would it feel like brushing his chest as she rode him? Tickling his thighs as she sucked him off? He swallowed and moved to massage the little hollows behind her neck. She sighed and her muscles became relaxed and pliant for him. He moved to her shoulders and worked at the knots there. He wasn't surprised she was riddled with them. She'd been kidnapped following a very annoying visit from that bastard her father called a suitor, and found out the people she took care of in the District were probably dead. She blamed herself. She needed a bit of pampering and to be told that their deaths weren't her fault. The government had exterminated them on a whim.

You want to touch her and see if you can coax her into riding your cock.

His hands trailed lower as he relaxed her muscles. He reached her ass and hesitated. He could make out the pert shape of it through the loosely draped t-shirt. Round and firm. He wanted to bite it. He ran his palm down the curve of it.

"Galen." Her voice held a smoky and seductive under current. She cleared her throat and it was gone. "You should stop."

Damn. "Right, of course."

"Shouldn't you go back to your own room?"

He began massaging her back instead. She'd been close to giving in to him, maybe he needed a little more time. *You're a bastard. Leave the woman alone.* It didn't stop his hands from continuing to roam her body.

"This isn't your room. It's mine. You'll be sleeping in here with me."

She rolled onto her back and his hands settled on her hips. "What the hell are you talking about?"

"It's either that or a holding cell. I figured you'd be happier here."

She shoved his hands off her. "Fine, where are you going to sleep?"

"Right next to you. In this bed."

"Oh, hell no!" She slid off the end of the bed, and as she moved past him he caught the scent of her wet pussy. She wanted him.

"Yes. Like I said, it's either this or spending your days in a cell. We're both adults. We can share a bed without having sex."

She snorted. "I can't even lie on the damned thing without you having your damned hands all over me."

He smirked. "Well, you could have stopped me at any time. I notice you didn't."

"A mistake I won't make again."

Way to go, dumbass. Point that out so she never lets you near her. "I won't touch you again." A lie. "Besides, you don't get a choice in the matter. Our jail isn't comfortable. They're cold, there's no shower or bed. You'll be comfortable here."

"Why can't I have my own room?"

"Because I don't trust you not to attempt escape once you figure out how everything works. Don't bother to deny that you would try. I know you."

"Ha! You don't."

"I know you well enough to determine this. You don't have a choice, so why don't you climb back into bed and get some sleep. I'm going to."

He stood and shucked his clothes with efficiency. The only thing he left on was his boxers. He flopped on the bed. He could feel her eyes on him the whole time and he rolled onto his back. He folded his arms behind his head and watched her stare at him.

"Like what you see?"

She glanced down and shuffled to the other side of the palette. She settled next to him, facing away. He sighed as she curled into a ball and the distinct clatter of teeth banging together reached his ears.

"Are you cold? I can adjust the temperature."

"I'm fine," she growled.

He raised the heat in the room by a few degrees using his connection to the ship. She'd likely never admit she was uncomfortable, and he didn't want her to freeze. Cyborgs kept the ship warm enough so they didn't catch hypothermia and die in space. Otherwise it was considered a waste of energy and a luxury to keep the ship warm. He wrapped an arm around her waist and pulled her into his body. She tensed so hard he thought she might strain something.

"Just until the room and mattress heat up. You're cold. I can hear your teeth chattering. Get some sleep."

He threw a leg over hers and forced them to straighten slightly. He kept it there so he was pressed more fully against her. Only his computer exerting inhuman control over his body kept his erection from surging to life.

He closed his eyes and drifted off to sleep.

Chapter Nine

She rocked against the solid object between her thighs as it bumped against her clit. Teeth scraped the back of her neck. Rough palms skimmed her belly before cupping her breasts. She'd dreamed of this. His hands on her, his mouth on her. She'd woken wet. Or maybe she hadn't dreamed it. Maybe he'd touched her first. She wasn't sure. She glanced over her shoulder.

"Hmm…what are you up to?"

He pressed his mouth to hers and thrust his tongue into her mouth, mimicking the rhythm of his thigh between her legs.

When he pulled away, she shook her head and tried to gain her focus back. "You don't fight fair."

"The last thing I want to do is fight with you. Aren't you tired of arguing? All that sexual tension must be building, and building." He skimmed one hand down her body to skim over her mound. He parted the folds of her sex and rubbed his finger against her clit.

She laughed and it came out shaky. "That's really…oh, Galen."

She was half asleep, and lacked the willpower to argue with him while he was touching her there. His tongue swept over her shoulder before he bit her lightly. She gasped as more warm wetness flooded her sex.

"I think you like this. You're all slippery. I want to have my tongue where I have my fingers. I can't wait to taste you again. You're like a drug."

She snorted. "Pretty words, but you don't mean them."

He chuckled. "Oh, I mean every word. You're beautiful here." He thrust two fingers into her vagina while his thumb continued to play with her clit. "You taste good, and I love the way you respond to me. I can't wait to have my hard cock sliding into your warm, tight body." He slowly pumped his fingers in and out of her cunt. "So tight. You need to get laid."

She was supposed to be protesting this. She should be fighting him. He was getting too close and eventually he'd betray her.

Her inner muscles tightened, little sparks of pleasure shooting up her spine, and he pulled away. She moaned in frustration. "What are you doing? Why did you stop?"

She grabbed the nape of his neck and pulled him into a scorching kiss. She ran her hand over his abs down to his dick and rubbed it through the cloth of his underwear. His sharp intake of breath broke their kiss.

"So demanding. I like that in a woman."

"Shut up."

He laughed and pulled her up, whipping her t-shirt over her head. "Gods, you have beautiful breasts. Large, bigger than handfuls." He shoved her back on the bed and held himself above her. She glanced down before wrapping her hands around his large, swollen cock. He growled low in his throat. "If you keep stroking me, this isn't going to last as long as you'd like."

She giggled and released him. "Okay, have it your way."

"I like your attitude. I intend to have you my way."

He lowered his hips to hers. He grasped his cock and stroked it up and down her wet folds, concentrating on her clit. She rocked herself against it. "Now, Galen, please. I want you inside me."

He flashed her a crooked grin and ran his dick around the entrance of her vagina. He slowly pressed himself inside. Her inner muscles stretched deliciously to accommodate him. He was almost too large. If she'd been less aroused, it would have been painful.

He lowered his head and pulled a nipple into his mouth as he worked his thick length farther into her cunt. He bit her breast lightly and she gasped, arching her hips against his. His arousal slid in all the way and he held himself still above her as he toyed with her breast.

She gasped and rocked her hips, but it wasn't enough to get her off. "Galen, stop teasing."

He slowly drew himself out, and hammered back into her. She cried out and he froze. "Are you okay?"

She looked at him. Really looked at him. His muscles were bulging with tension, his brow furrowed with concentration as he watched her. He was worried about hurting her.

"I want you to fuck me hard." She wrapped her legs around his hips and yanked them to hers.

He didn't need more encouragement. He thrust in and out of her at a punishing pace. Her breath came in gasps as he pounded into her.

"God, I'm not going to last," he groaned.

He slid his hands down her body and found her clit, wiggling his fingers over the sensitive flesh. Pleasure bloomed in her cunt and she shouted as she shook apart from her orgasm.

Galen thrust into her one last time as he shouted her name. His heated cum shot into her as his elbows sagged. He didn't let himself collapse on her, which she was grateful for; he'd crush her.

He rolled them over so she was sprawled on top of him and they tried to catch their breath.

"You know…there's no trophy above this bed."

He chuckled. "Yeah, that was bullshit."

"Huh. That's unfortunate. It might have gotten you laid sooner."

He snorted and squeezed her to his chest. They stayed like that in silence for a long while. She started to fade into sleep when he whispered, "I am sorry for bringing you here. I shouldn't be. I shouldn't give a damn, but you didn't deserve the threats of death."

She traced a circle around his nipple. "You're far from forgiven, but thanks for that. Don't hurt me again."

He sighed, and stroked her back, but he didn't promise not to betray her. He didn't say anything.

$$\bullet \ \bullet \ \bullet$$

The crackle of the intercom brought Jamila out of her half sleep. She blinked and rubbed her eyes.

"Galen, report to meeting room one."

He groaned. "No. Shut up, Torin."

A male chuckle came over the com. "Come on, man. Council wants the lowdown on your mission. Don't make me come get you."

"Ugh, fuck you."

"You know I'm not comfortable with your homosexual tendencies. Find a different boyfriend."

Jamila slid off him and poked his side. "Get up."

"Oooh, did you get laid?"

"I'm going to kill you, Torin."

Torin's snort was so loud that she jumped. "I guess not. Sex is supposed to make you more relaxed."

She poked him again and kept at it. "Get up. I've never known you to be a stubborn riser."

He opened one eye to regard her. "That's because I didn't sleep while I stayed with you. I was hoping to make up for that before I have a mental breakdown."

She snickered. "Like you'd ever have a mental breakdown." She brought her knees to her chest and pushed at him with her feet, trying to shove him out of bed. "Get up. You're gonna get in trouble."

"Torin, I blame you for this. She's kicking me."

She pushed with her feet and slid away from him instead of moving him. "Oh, hush. I can't move you anyway. You weigh five million pounds."

A bark of laughter exploded over the com.

He glared at the ceiling. "Computer, shut down communications." There was a click, and then silence.

He rolled over, grabbed her ankles, and pulled her under him. She squeaked as he pinned her with his hips.

"I was hoping to have sex again before I had to go anywhere."

She smirked. "I don't think you have time. Torin sounded like he was going to come get you now if you don't show, and I'd rather not be in the middle of a mind-blowing orgasm when he gets here. Or worse yet, not getting that orgasm before you have to go."

He snorted. "Right. He does tend to barge in without signaling. That might be embarrassing for all involved." He grumbled. "Great. I get to go into this meeting with a very obvious hard on."

She laughed and shook her head. "Poor thing."

He flopped onto his back and took a few breaths before standing and dressing. "I'll send someone to watch you while I'm gone. They'll go get you food or something."

"Coffee would be appreciated."

He grimaced. "Sorry, no coffee. Why do you think I was knocking it back while I was at your house? We have this one drink that is supposed to mimic it. It mimics the caffeine content, but the taste…Saying it leaves much to be desired is an understatement."

She glared at him. "You know, kidnapping me is one thing, but not giving me coffee? Are you trying to get me to kill you? Because I'll do it."

"I'm trembling."

"You should be. A woman's coffee should not be taken away."

"Duly noted. Hopefully when we get to the station I can find you some. We're a little better supplied there."

They'd better be, or she was going to lose a lot of weight. The food had been horrible. She didn't know how anyone ate that stuff. She felt cruel for giving it to the orphans for the past year. A sharp page of sadness hit her heart. She would never get a chance to get them anything better.

"Okay. I'll be back in like an hour. Torin will be down to sit with you in a few minutes, so don't freak out when he comes through the door. And uh, put some clothes on, because he's a horn dog. I have shorts in a drawer that have a drawstring that will probably work for bottoms. I'll be sure to get your clothes cleaned."

She nodded and he stepped out of the apartment. She rolled out of bed and pulled on the shirt he'd divested her of last night. The door hissed open and Galen strode back in.

"Did you forget something?"

"Yes." He tangled his hands in her hair and pressed his lips to hers in a drugging kiss. He pulled away and kissed her forehead before he left. She couldn't help but grin.

She shook her head. He might be sweet now, but he hadn't said he wouldn't betray her again, which told her something important. His plan involved things that could hurt her or her father. She liked him a lot, but she couldn't let him get to her. It could be devastating if he did. She'd already slipped and ended up in his bed.

She glanced around the room. He was right about one thing. She did plan to try and escape when he wasn't around. She didn't know how much time she had before Torin showed up, but she had better get to work before he arrived. She didn't dare ask the computer where the life pods were. She was probably being monitored. However, she could manually access the ship's systems if they hadn't shut down control. She wouldn't put it past them to shut down manual input. Not with the way she'd seen Galen interact with electronics. He seemed to be able to control most things with his mind.

But she could hope. She grabbed some shorts from the drawer Galen had left open and pulled them on as she scanned the room for an access panel. It wasn't hard to guess where it would be. There was a visual communications terminal on the desk across from the bed. She slipped into the chair next to it, and found exactly what she was searching for. She ran her finger over the touch screen and nodded in approval when it lit up.

She accessed the ship's schematics and easily located the life pods. The closest ones were four decks below her. How could one unattended human make it there? That was the question. The ship had been teaming with cyborgs when she'd come aboard. She'd seem out of place, to be sure.

But she had to give it a shot. If she could launch, she could head for the nearest inhabited world, far away from the Edge. Far away from Galen and his scheming.

She walked to the door but it didn't slide open automatically like it did for Galen. This ship was state of the art. All the doors would open when someone approached unless they were programmed not to, or locked. Maybe he'd had it changed for privacy. She could hope, anyway.

"Computer, open the door."

She got no response from it and the doors stayed closed. "Computer, respond."

Silence. She glared at the door and searched for the access panel. He must have reprogrammed the computer to not accept her voice.

"Dammit. What now?" She paced in front of the door and tried to come up with a plan.

"Computer, emergency release. There's a fire."

The door slid open, revealing the hulking, grinning blond who had grabbed her at her house before she could escape. She jumped, and took a step back.

"Watcha doin'?"

She backed into the room. "Nothing."

Torin rolled his eyes. "I believe you."

She crossed her arms over her chest. "I'm sure you do. Don't I have a trustworthy face?"

His laughter told her no. He stepped in and the door closed behind him, cutting off her escape.

"You know, running off isn't the best idea. Life outside a core planet isn't easy. Even people who are normally decent will take advantage of the possession of a senator's daughter. A life pod wouldn't be in range of anything but dangerous backwater rocks that the core planets export their criminals to."

Nice try. Even a "backwater rock" with criminals on it would have military personnel. "I wasn't planning to—"

"Don't bullshit me, Jamila. Five seconds with you and I already know you're a bad liar."

She paced away from him. "So I should stay here and let Galen use me to get what he wants? And he'll kill me if he doesn't get his way? I can't say that sounds like a good plan."

"Trust me. It's better than going out there. I don't think you understand the dangers. Pirates. Slavers—both human and alien. And sometime the aliens will blow your ship out of the sky. It really depends on the captain. You don't want to run into Corabin slavers. I mean, humans are bad, but the Corabin? You'd never see home again. At least Galen will take you back some day."

"Did you miss the killing me part?"

He smirked. "I find that incredibly unlikely. Especially since the room smells like sex. He can be cold blooded, but I think he likes you a little more than that."

"And this Council you spoke of?"

Torin grimaced and she could almost see the wheels turning in his head as he debated what exactly he should tell her. "The Council isn't a big fan of humans. They like your father even less."

She frowned. "Why? What has he done to them?"

He bit his lip, tilting his head. His eyes narrowed. "That's a long story, and something I probably shouldn't tell you."

"How am I supposed to understand if no one ever tells me what's going on?"

He smiled. "There's a reason. They're not my tales to tell. And you're so young, Galen probably feels like he can't tell you anything. You're a child."

She rolled her eyes. "He's not that much older than me."

"He's forty. And even if he weren't his life experience would make him older."

She gaped at him. "Forty? He doesn't look it."

His smile disappeared. "Yeah, well, we don't seem to be aging. He appears and feels the age they accelerated him to in the labs. Which I guess is nice, since they took about ten years off his life if he'd kept aging."

"Wait, back up. Accelerated aging? Explain."

"You didn't know that about us? They watch the lower class settlements, and choose children or teenagers they think are exemplary. They pick them young because they're easier to mold and brainwash. But they can't do anything with children. They don't have enough strength and they look too conspicuous if they're spotted on missions so they're growth is accelerated. Galen was seventeen if I remember right."

"And how old were you?"

He shook his head. "I was six."

"Wow, I'm surprised they could reform you. I'd think you'd be completely devoted to the government, if they brainwashed you."

All humor left him and alarm bells went off in her head. This man wasn't as stable as he seemed. "Oh, it was hard for them to fix me. And now they have to deal with my depression and suicidal tendencies. The government fucks up every life they touch. Including Galen's. You're lucky he doesn't treat you like shit. If I didn't find you amusing, or see the change in him, I would try to kill you myself."

She gulped and stepped back against the door. "Galen wouldn't like that."

His tight lipped smile wasn't a happy one. "No, he wouldn't. That's why you're safe, until he starts to hate you. Which I find inevitable. Humans always show their true colors eventually."

"May I remind you that you're human."

His eyes narrowed. "No, we're not. We were born human, but they changed us. They fucked us up. And your father was a big part of that."

"My father is a senator. He has very little active access to that part of the government. They regulate it, but even they don't have all the facts."

"He wasn't always a senator, was he? What was he doing, say thirty years ago? Twenty even?"

She didn't have a clue. What was he accusing him of? She bit her lip, not wanting to acknowledge her ignorance of her father to this man.

"You don't know, do you? Because I know exactly what he was up to. We all do."

She put her hands on her hips. "Well, out with it. Tell me why you hate me."

"Now, now. Don't put words in my mouth. I find you... interesting. I hate your father, and believe you'll turn out to be his daughter through and through. He was an experimental psychiatrist where they were making us. He conducted everything to do with the brainwashing. We can't help but blame him for our lives. He changed us. Our lives suck because of him. We're not looking forward to dealing with him when we think he should be assassinated."

Jamila glanced away from him, her mind reeling. She had no idea her father had a hand in creating cyborgs. Galen could never love her. Her father had done too many terrible things to him. In ways, she looked a lot like him. Every time he stared into her eyes, did he cringe and think of the pain her father had caused him? Was that why when they'd met, he couldn't seem to regard her with anything but contempt?

A good way to hurt her father would be to murder her. Galen must know that. She needed to escape this ship and risk the trip back. There was no doubt in her mind now that she'd end up dead if she stayed. Her father wouldn't bow to Galen's commands, and these people were bent on revenge against him. She could see it in Torin's eyes. She was a pawn to them and she needed to find a way out.

"Any chance you can get me some food? I'd rather not go to the mess hall. I was threatened last time I went there."

Torin laughed. "Yeah, that bitch Ann thinks she owns Galen's cock now. She gets like that sometimes. I'll go out and get you food. She hates humans and would definitely make good on any threats."

The doors slid open automatically as he approached them and left. When they slipped closed again, she moved to stand in front of them but they didn't budge. She wasn't surprised. He'd be stupid to leave them unlocked, but it was worth a shot. She glanced around for a weapon. She didn't want to kill him, just knock him out. There was nothing in here. It was like a person didn't even live in this room. Galen was either a neat freak or owned no personal items.

There had to be weapon in here. There was no way he'd be without. Space was dangerous. It was full of pirates and aliens and he was a fugitive from his own government. A ship could easily be boarded silently, and you might never know it until someone spotted the intruder and sounded the alarm, or they broke into your room and tried to kill you.

The one strange thing she spotted was a keypad next to the head of the bed on the left side. She rushed to the bed and dived on it, scrambling for the other side. Some ships had safety boxes in the cabins to protect valuables. The only thing different about this one was that the symbols on the keys were like nothing she'd ever seen before. Had cyborgs created their own written language as well as a spoken one? She probably wouldn't have been able to figure out the code even if she could recognize the signs.

She wiggled her fingernails under the plastic keypad and tried to work it loose. She gritted her teeth as the dull throb of her nails threatening to pull from her fingers became more insistent. There was a small pop and she flinched, waiting for agony. Instead, the small plastic frame and keypad dropped to the floor.

She examined the wires under the buttons. *You're going to electrocute yourself.* Rubbing her hands together she considered them. Her inner skeptic had a point. It had been years since she'd had training in electronics. Thankfully, unless Galen had booby trapped this panel, it was unlikely to give her a fatal jolt. She tugged a wire from the center and it came loose with minimal effort. When she combined it with a wire from the bottom of the panel sparks flew from the entire thing. White hot pain hit her fingers sending tingles up her arms and she landed on her ass. She shook her head and took a deep breath, trying to get rid of the shaky feeling the shock left her with. The good news? A large square of the wall was open ever so slightly. That wasn't how she preferred to get his vault open, but it would do.

Jamila pushed herself to her feet, and stumbled to the wall. She swung the door of the safe open and almost cheered when she spotted what was inside. She couldn't believe her luck. It was a stun gun.

Sinking into a chair behind the desk, she examined the stunner. She wasn't sure how to use one. She'd only seen it done. But she'd been told it was only a matter of "point and shoot." She hoped that was the case. Normal pistols had a safety. If the little stun gun had one she was screwed.

She slid it between her knees and waited for Torin to come back. Hopefully he wouldn't take forever. She would love to stand and pace, but that would probably arouse his suspicion. That was the last thing she needed. She had no idea what Torin might do to her if he discovered she was trying to escape. He wouldn't be happy.

The door slid open and Torin stepped through carrying a tray. She lifted the stunner and fired. His eyes widened as the beam struck him.

"Fuck…" His eyes rolled back in his head and he sank to his knees before collapsing onto his stomach. The tray clattered on the ground and she flinched. If anyone had heard or seen that, she wasn't going to make it anywhere. She rushed to the door and peered out. There was no one in the hall. Yet. She needed to shove him into the room. She got on her knees and pushed his legs through the door. It would have been so much easier to pull the big bastard, but the doors would likely slide closed once he was inside, and that wouldn't do. She struggled to get his heavy legs to move.

"Damned cyborgs must weigh eight hundred pounds. Good lord." They did have reinforced skeletons, but the metal was supposed to be light. But after this she knew it couldn't possibly be as light as everyone said. Or maybe this was how much people weighed. She'd never had to push an unconscious man through a doorway before.

She finally managed to get his legs through the door and rested for a second against the frame. His eyes flickered open and she jumped.

"Don't do this." His voice was so low she could barely make out his words. "You'll be in terrible danger. Don't leave."

"I have no choice. I'm convinced I'm going to end up dead. At the very least you're going to use me for your own personal gain." She snorted. "Besides, once you're able to get up, you're going to be pissed. I can't stay now."

His hand clenched and then his eyes fell closed. Cyborgs were resilient. She'd never seen anyone wake so soon after they'd been shot with a stunner. The majority were out for at least fifteen minutes. Now she had only one problem. The door to Galen's room hadn't closed. Torin might have been awake enough to keep it from shutting. She couldn't know for sure. It didn't matter. She had to go.

She stood and rushed down the hall. Thanks to the glance she'd gotten of the layout of the ship, she could easily find her way to an escape pod. It was four levels down. She made it to the lift without being spotted by anyone. She hit the button for the level she needed and waited.

The lift ground to a halt before she'd reached her destination. A cyborg stepped into the elevator with her. He frowned but quickly pressed the button to get them moving again. He glanced down at her and took a breath like he would say something, but then he abruptly faced forward again, clasping his right wrist with his left hand. Did he suspect where she was going and why? Did he even know who she was? They couldn't have many humans in this place. He didn't look at her again and for that she was grateful.

Chapter Ten

Jamila stepped out of the elevator when they reached her level. When she glanced behind her, the man was watching her. He wasn't intense about it, but he was definitely tracking her movements. She walked past the entrance to the life pod and kept going, waiting for the telltale whisper of the lift doors closing. When she heard it, she glanced behind her to check. Yep, he was on his way. She turned around and rushed toward the pod. She needed to hurry.

"What are you doing down here, human?"

Jamila froze and slowly turned to face the last woman she wanted to see. Ann strode toward her with her hands on her hips. Where had that bitch come from? And the real question: what was she going to do now? She had no answer for Ann, and even if she did, this woman still wanted to pound on her a little bit. Or a lot.

"Answer me. What are you doing down here without an escort?"

Jamila's mind scrambled for an excuse. She found none and her words tripped off her tongue. "I…I was going to the cargo bay. I left something in the shuttle. Galen allowed it."

The biggest lie ever. Could a cyborg detect a lie? Probably. If they paid attention even normal people could notice some of the signs.

Ann's eyes narrowed and she was sure she'd been caught. Then a chilling smile broke across Ann's face that made her stomach flip over with anxiety.

"I'm glad you're alone. We can talk. Woman to woman. Let me be very clear. Galen is mine, and I want you to keep your hands off him."

Jamila flinched internally. Clearly Ann wasn't close enough to scent him. Jamila hadn't showered; she must still smell like him. She backed away, hoping to keep out of the range of Ann's cyborg super nose.

"You don't even deserve to live. I'm going to push for your execution when your father doesn't meet our demands, which I'm sure he won't. No humans should survive for what they've done to us."

Jamila cleared her tight throat. "You know you're still human, right? No matter how much you've been transformed. You're sounding a little crazy." She shook her head. *Moron. Antagonize the wacky, jealous cyborg. It's one of your better plans lately.* She bumped against the opposite wall and cringed as Ann kept advancing, her hands curled into fists.

"Be careful, bitch. We don't need you alive to complete our mission. It makes things easier, but it shouldn't be required." Then she froze and her eyes narrowed. "You little whore. You've slept with him already!" Her lip curled. "But then, from the videos we've seen of you, you always were a slut."

She charged forward and Jamila realized she should have stunned her as soon as she'd been spotted. She was too close now, and Jamila was either going to die, or take a few nasty blows before she could take her down. If she pulled the stunner now, Ann would take it from her. She'd lose her chance to incapacitate her and end up dead. Fear quivered in her gut. Would she even survive one blow? Probably not.

Ann backhanded her. She fell to her knees and black spots danced in front of her vision. If Ann had closed her fist it would have killed her.

A hand tangled in her hair while the other clamped around her bicep hard enough to bruise. Her stomach turned over as Ann tossed her. She threw her arms around her head as she crashed into the wall. Her ribs lit up with pain and she cried out. She bounced off it and hit the ground on her side.

She blinked and fought against the blackness that threatened to pull her under. She fumbled for the stunner in the back of her pants. Her trembling hands wrapped around it and her fuzzy vision cleared enough to see Ann storming toward her. She raised her weapon and fired.

Ann collapsed five feet from her. Jamila pushed herself to her feet and leaned against the wall as a wave of dizziness swamped her. She braced her hands on her knees and took a couple of deep breaths before she stumbled to the escape pods. She couldn't halt her shaking. She was lucky to be alive. Nausea rolled through her stomach and she wasn't sure if it had to do with fear or a concussion.

She stepped through the little door and glanced around. It was spacious, with enough room for several people. And each one was supposed to have enough oxygen for a month of space travel. With only one person, she could last much longer. Hopefully she wouldn't need that long. There were supposed to be food rations somewhere in it too.

Sitting in the pilot's chair, she glanced around at the controls. They were much simpler than her shuttle back home. But then, navigation wasn't a big need in an escape pod. It would head for the nearest government controlled planet or space station. If that was unavailable, it would head for the nearest habitable world.

"Computer, prepare for launch."

"Negative."

"What? Prepare for launch now and head for the following coordinates." She imputed the destination manually.

"Negative."

Crap. She really couldn't deal with this now. She couldn't think straight. Her face and ribs ached and she couldn't halt her trembling. "This ship is under attack. I need to go."

"Negative."

She groaned. What the hell was wrong with this thing? She stared at the controls. They gave no hint that it was malfunctioning. She input the command to lift off manually. The only response it gave was two loud buzzing sounds.

She screamed and kicked the underside of the dash, cursing when her toes throbbed from the impact.

"Computer, reason for non-compliance?"

"Command controls have been remotely overridden."

A chill went down her spine. "By who?"

"Oh, I think you know who."

She spun around to find Galen leaning against the shuttle's doorway. She hadn't even realized the damned thing hadn't closed. She pulled the little stun gun out of her pocket and pointed it at his chest. He arched an eyebrow. "Really now?"

"Yes, really. I've had enough and I'm leaving. Let me go or I'll—"

"Stun me? Oooh, what a threat that is. The ship still won't lift off without my order." He eased closer and she tensed, ready to stun him. He froze. "How badly are you injured? Let me look at you."

She shook her head as tears clouded her vision. "No, stay away from me. I'm tired of being hurt by you people."

Her eyes narrowed. Had he hacked the other pods too? She could stun him and still get away.

"I know what you're thinking. The answer is yes. I've hacked the other pods. Even if I hadn't, the cyborg you encountered in the lift noticed you. He mentioned that he'd spotted a human when he went past me."

"How did you know I'd escaped?"

He snorted. "The more I thought about where I left the pistol, the more I worried that I was underestimating you, so I went back to remove it from my cabin. And of course you know what I found. A barely conscious, pissed, cursing Torin, trying to pull himself to the communications terminal. He was relieved to see me. I guessed where you'd gone. This was the closest evac spot. And Ann lying unconscious in the corridor was a good sign too."

He strode toward her and she wiggled the stunner to get his attention. He paused. "It doesn't matter. Go ahead and shoot me. When I wake up, you'll be locked up somewhere and I'll be plenty pissed. Should be fun to take that frustration out on you." More tears formed in her eyes and his widened. "Shit. Okay not the tact to take right now. Please, let me look at you."

She glared at him. She wanted to drop her guard. Needed a shoulder to cry on. But she wasn't staying here one more minute.

"What was the plan anyway? I know you're aware there are pirates and aliens and all sorts of problems you could run in to. And you probably wouldn't have made it far from us. They would have launched the Wingmen to disable your engines and tow you back. Those guys are good at that kind of thing. If you did get away, you'd probably get killed."

She bared her teeth at him. "I'm not sure I won't end up dead if I stay here. Psycho bitch in the hallway tried to kill me. The best way to hurt my father would be to kill me if you don't get your way. You people hate him."

His expression grew stern. "Stop saying 'you people' like that. It's not like you to generalize. It smacks of prejudice. You don't honestly think I'd hurt you, do you? I didn't think I'd be able to bluff you this easily."

"Yes, well, maybe I've been mistreated enough that I'm entitled. I used to think your people were decent, and unfairly treated. Now I can't be sure." And she didn't believe him. He would likely have no problem hurting her. He'd said it. He'd told her that was the plan if her father didn't comply. "You're trying to confuse me."

He sighed and shook his head. Then he sprang forward with a burst of speed and knocked the stun gun out of her hand before she had a chance to fire. He grabbed her and hauled her out of the chair. He dragged her backward and tossed her on the floor of the shuttle, careful not to hurt her in the fall or crush her as he came down on top of her.

"Gods, but you frustrate me. I don't think I could ever hurt you, and damn me for the weakness. I'll keep you safe. The threat of you being hurt will be enough to convince your father to help us. I won't need to do more. And if he rejects our proposition then you'll stay here. He'll assume we killed you or are torturing you. We never have to do it, and more importantly I'll make sure no one does. Ann will be kept far from you."

"I don't trust you. You betrayed me. I don't want to stay here forever. I want to go home."

He sighed and rested his forehead against hers. "You don't understand. You'll see why we need you when we get to the station. I can't believe you don't understand. You saw what the government did to that Haven district. Besides, if I hadn't taken you, you probably would have been arrested. You'll see."

She shook her head. "I still don't believe you won't hurt me. You've proved you're a liar."

He reared back like she'd slapped him. "That you even think I could hurt you proves you don't know me."

"How can I? You don't tell me anything. And you know everything about me. You show no emotion."

His eyes narrowed. "Right."

His lips met hers with frenzied need. The kiss was possessive, demanding, and left her completely dazed. He grabbed the back of one of her knees and spread her thighs so he was cradled between them. She shoved at his chest and he broke the kiss.

"Kissing me, sex, it doesn't prove anything."

His lips slid over her racing pulse. "You don't think so? It means a lot to me. I crave you. I always want to touch you. You keep surprising me in the best ways. I enjoy spending time with you. Even when you argue with me."

It wasn't a declaration of love, but it was almost everything but. It was touching.

"I will never let anyone hurt you."

His teeth scraped across her throat and little shivers shot down her spine.

He pulled her shirt over her head and hissed. She glanced down and saw that her right side was already starting to bruise. She didn't feel it. Maybe she was still running on adrenaline.

"Ann did that."

He growled. "I figured. I'm going to kill her."

Running his hand down her body, he tweaked her nipple playfully before placing his palm on her ribs. She flinched as he pressed down and he nodded. "Well, if anything was broken, that would have caused screaming. Don't worry, when we're done here, I'll be taking you to medical to fix all this."

She shrugged. "It's just a few bruises."

He snorted and kissed her throat. "It won't feel like just a few bruises in an hour."

He skimmed his fingers down her belly before deftly unfastening her pants and pressing the heel of his palm against her sex. He stroked her in slow, maddening circles.

"Stop." She couldn't let him keep going. If she gave into him he'd keep her here. She wanted to trust him, but he'd betrayed her, threatened her, and she'd been assaulted by Ann. And she would probably be killed by his government no matter what he wanted.

He ran his tongue over the hollow under her ear. "No. I plan to convince you to stay and I can't do that if I don't put my hands all over you."

She gasped as he lightly pinched her clit between his fingers. "You could talk to me to try to persuade me."

He nipped her collarbone. "This is much easier, and more enjoyable. You can't deny that. Besides, I'm pissed that you tried to leave, and pounding my frustration out in you definitely appeals."

Her pussy clenched at his words as she imagined him riding her hard.

He chuckled. "I think you like the sound of that."

His hands left her pants and he seized the waistband, tugging them down. She kicked her feet to shake them off, eager to have him now, consequences be damned.

She ran her hands up his chest, unhooking his uniform as she went before pushing it off his broad shoulders. He growled as she captured his nipple between her teeth. He shoved his suit down his hips enough that his cock sprang free into her waiting hands.

He captured her wrists. "No, turn over. On your hands and knees. Now."

Her eyes narrowed at his demanding tone and she opened her mouth to argue.

"Unless you want me to spank you, which I'm already considering, you'll do what I say."

She bit her lip and tried to stifle the thrill of anticipation as she turned over and rose to her hands and knees.

He groaned like he was being tortured and groped her ass. "This sight could not get more perfect."

She shuddered as he caressed her lower back and shifted her thighs farther apart.

"Do you want me to take you?"

She nodded. "Yes."

"Even if it won't solve anything?"

She rolled her eyes. Trust him to throw that back in her face now. "I really don't care." She only knew she wanted him.

The harsh slap of flesh hitting flesh filled her ears and her ass cheek burned. Anger and arousal blended and she tried to sit up. He easily held her in place.

"I didn't think you were serious about that spanking."

"Then you still don't understand what danger you were in if you left here."

He smacked her again and she yelped. "Stop that."

"Tell me you'll never try to escape again."

She hesitated and his hand landed on her ass again.

"Say it," he ground out.

Indignation sparked through her. She wasn't a two-year-old. She knew what she was doing. It might have been dangerous but so was staying here. She opened her mouth to argue and flinched when he smacked her again.

She nodded and gasped, "Fine. I won't try to leave again."

He sighed and rested some of his weight on her. He ran his palm up her spine and tangled it in her hair before kissing the back of her neck.

She rocked back against his hips and his erection bumped her ass. "Please screw me now, Galen."

He growled. "God, that's what I love to hear."

He rubbed back and forth, wetting his dick on her pussy, driving her wild, before he pressed slowly into her cunt. She whimpered and rocked against him but he grabbed her hips and held her still.

"Hard and fast, Galen."

He slammed into her and she moaned his name as he gave her what she wanted. His strength was almost painful, his pace punishing. He rubbed her clit in small circular motions, in time with his thrusts, and warm pleasure bloomed in her vagina. She gasped his name as her pussy clenched around him. He didn't stop thrusting and her back bowed with the rapture of her second orgasm.

He gave one final thrust and shouted her name as his seed jetted inside of her. He collapsed over her, taking them both to the ground. He rolled off of her before he crushed her.

They lay side by side on the cold floor for a while. She wasn't sure how long they stayed like that, but eventually the intercom buzzed.

Galen groaned. "Computer, broadcast audio."

"Galen, Alec's ship showed. I know you're waiting for him."

Galen sat up. "Dress," he said in a low voice before raising it to speak with the person on the com. "Anyone with him?"

"You have no idea. He had to pack them in like sardines. There were more than we expected."

She frowned at him. "More what?"

He flapped his hand at her, signaling her to be quiet. "That's good to hear."

"Ah, so you caught the little witch. You're going to pay for stunning me, Jamila."

She flinched and glanced at Galen. He rolled his eyes and shook his head. "Don't worry about it."

"She'd better worry."

He glared at the com. "Torin, let it go." He glanced at her. "Come on. You'll want to see this."

He grabbed her hand once she'd finished closing her pants and pulled her out of the jumper to the lift. They went down a few more levels to shuttle bay. Galen's tension was palpable. She could even feel it in the way he held her hand.

The elevator jolted to a halt and he dragged her out as the doors slid open. The bay was teaming with people. Their clothes were tattered. They were bruised. Most were huddled together, too afraid to explore their surroundings while others were laid out on the ground being tended by others.

She glanced at Galen. "Who are these people? Where is your doctor? Some need medical care."

He squeezed her hand. "Don't worry for them. The medical staff has been summoned."

A deeply tanned cyborg marched around the bay, his voice booming above the din. "Get repair crews down here once we clear out the wounded. We barely made it back. Damn Galen and his persistence."

"Fuck you, Alec," Galen yelled across to him, but the small smile on his face said he didn't mean it.

Alec waved at him.

"Jamila?" After the first shout a chorus of voices called her name. She glanced around, releasing Galen's hand and stepping away. She couldn't find where the shouts were coming from, but it didn't take her long to notice a small group of children hurdling toward her, Jackson in the lead.

She dropped to her knees as he crashed into her followed by several other wiggling bodies.

The chorus of voices shouted questions at her in rapid fire. She couldn't even begin to decipher them. Alice and Darion rushed up behind the kids.

Darion shouted, "Quiet! Geez, let the woman take a breath so you can ask your questions one at a time."

They quieted and glanced at Darion. Jamila stood, separating herself from the squirming children, and rushed to hug Alice and Darion.

"I can't believe you're alive. How?" She glanced at Galen and he shrugged.

Darion clasped her hand. "Not everyone was killed. As you can see, some were captured as they tried to flee the bombs. We actually hid in a tunnel under the house with several others, and when the bombing was over we tried to sneak out of the tunnels and we were captured. They were taking us on a ship to the Capital where we were supposed to be interrogated and disposed of."

Alice glanced at Galen. "He had us saved, I'm told. Thank you. It wasn't fair to have these children's lives ended so young."

He nodded. "You'll be safe where we're going. I can't promise there won't be dangers, but we're all trying to make better lives for ourselves away from the prying eyes of the government. It's not easy but you'll be much better off."

She nodded. "Thank you. I can't express how grateful we are."

The burden of guilt pressed down on Jamila's heart and she flung her arms around the women again. "I'm so glad you're safe! I was heartbroken. The attack was my fault. I was careless with the last delivery. I—"

Galen's palms landed on her shoulders. "Hush now. It was probably something they'd been planning for months, if not years."

Alice shook her head and crossed her arms low over her stomach, hunching in on herself. "He's right. They never intended to let any of us survive for long. There were never any weapons being run into the district like they claimed. They were looking for an excuse to murder us, like they've wanted to do all along. It wasn't your fault, and we're so glad you weren't captured, because we heard them say they were going to arrest everyone involved. We assumed they'd already executed you if you weren't with us." Her eyes flickered to Galen. "We should have known you would save her."

He wrapped an arm around Jamila's shoulders and pulled her back against his chest. "Yes, you should have."

He nibbled her ear and she tossed him an annoyed glance over her shoulder. "That's not exactly what you did."

He grinned. "But I'll take the credit."

Darion cleared her throat. "Well, if you'll excuse us, we need to get the children settled. And some of them have injuries."

Galen pointed to Alec. "If you talk to him, you'll be the first he sets accommodations for. And he'll lead you somewhere to get you some food for all these starving squirts."

There was an uproar from the children at the mention of food and the women hustled them toward the captain.

Jamila turned in Galen's arms and stared up at him. She couldn't keep tears from blurring her vision. "You did this for me, didn't you?"

He nodded. "Of course. It was hard to miss your reaction when you discovered the attack on the district. If they were alive I had to save them. However, it wasn't only for you. It would be against everything we're trying to gain if we let those people go to their deaths. They needed saving, and luckily the mission was successful."

She pulled him down and kissed him lightly. "I can't believe you did this for me."

His arms tightened around her. "How could I not? You were so upset. It was worth it." He chuckled. "Though Alec might disagree."

She glanced over her shoulder and spotted the tanned man. He had one child on his shoulders, one wrapped around each leg, and one swinging from each hand. She giggled. "I think he would send them back if he could."

Galen wiggled his eyebrows. "But they're all his now. Along with women who will gladly kick his ass if he so much as frowns at one."

"You!" The harsh bark sounded across the cargo bay. Jamila spun around to see Torin eating the distance with long, angry strides.

She flinched and glanced at Galen who grinned down at her. "Nope, you have to deal with him. You pissed him off. He'll probably spank you."

She ran her finger down his chest. "I'd prefer if you did."

"Oh, I will again, but it won't get you out of this."

He spun her around and pushed her toward Torin. She gaped at him as he backed up. "Traitor," she hissed.

"No, he thinks I should get my revenge on you."

She gasped and stared at Torin, who'd reached her with alarming speed.

He crossed his arms over his chest. "Well, what do you have to say for yourself?"

She grinned at him. "Sorry?"

He growled at her and she jumped. "Okay, so I'm not sorry. I wanted to escape. What you said to me freaked me out and I wanted to leave."

Galen cleared his throat. "What exactly did you say to her, Torin?"

The frown creasing Torin's face told her that he'd been backed into a corner. He shifted restlessly on his feet. "There might have been something about the Council not liking humans, and the hand her father had in our creation. And maybe a tiny threat to her life."

"Torin!"

He bit his bottom lip. "I'd never actually hurt her. It was only a passing thought when I first met her. She's changed my mind. And I agree I shouldn't have told her what her father did, or what the Council would likely do to her. It slipped out in a fit of irrational anger."

Galen placed his hands on her shoulders and ran them down her arms. "The Council isn't going to do anything to her."

Torin nodded. "Of course not. We won't let them."

Jamila frowned at him. "So suddenly you like me?"

He grinned. "I have no choice. If I don't show my support, your boyfriend is going to pummel me for convincing you to take off."

Her gaze shifted to Galen. "Don't beat him up. It didn't take much convincing, and I was already looking for a way out when he came through the door."

Galen cleared his throat. "Torin, I need to talk to you for a second. Away from my prisoner."

Torin glanced at her. "Right."

Her eyes narrowed. What did they want to discuss that she couldn't be privy to? They stepped away and she crossed her arms over her chest, glaring at Galen. They were probably talking about her escape attempt. She sighed. Hopefully Galen would trust her not to do it again, but she'd probably ruined that. He'd probably punish her for it and not in the really great way he had in the pod.

Someone tapped her hard on the shoulder and she turned to see one of the refugees standing behind her. He was strangely clean and filled out for a man from Haven.

"Jamila Clearborne?"

"Yes?"

White hot pain pierced her chest stealing her breath. She glanced down and saw the knife planted in her sternum. She hit the ground on her knees as Galen shouted her name.

Chapter Eleven

His heart stopped. The assassin raised another knife. He was too close. Galen couldn't make it. He pushed his legs to the limit to make it across the cargo bay. Alec reached them first. He grasped the attacker's head and twisted. A crack filled the bay and Alec dropped the man.

Galen dropped to his knees and slid the last three feet to Jamila's side. He gathered her into his arms. She reached up and grasped the knife but he quickly stilled her hands.

"No, no, don't pull it out. It will bleed more."

She moved her hand to his cheek. "You're crying."

He swiped at his face. "I'm fine. You'll be okay. It's nothing."

She was going to die. Here in his arms after he'd promised he'd keep her safe. This was his fault. He shouldn't have let her out of his sight. Not with all these strangers in the room. What was wrong with him? He should have been here to take this blow for her. He knew she had enemies.

He took a deep breath. He needed to be strong for her now. "Are you in pain?"

She frowned. "No."

Torin knelt next to him. "Good. You'll be alright. Medic! Get over here now." Only years of working with Torin allowed Galen to detect the note of panic in the man's voice.

The doctor dropped down by them and pulled bandaging out of his bag. "Get me a gurney," he muttered absently as he packed cloth around the blade.

Jamila's eyes slipped shut as her pulse slowed under his fingers, and horror roared through his head. "Doc, she's dying. Do something!"

Torin cleared his throat and shifted his weight. "Galen, the wound is fatal. You know that."

The doctor grunted. "Fuck that. We can save her if we get creative."

Galen took his eyes off Jamila's still form. "What do you mean?"

"What do you think? We'll alter her. Replace her heart and accelerate her healing. Help me get her on the gurney—gently. I want her jostled as little as possible. We have to hurry."

The doctor supported her feet while Galen lifted her shoulders and set her on the gurney. The medical instruments came to life with the howls of alerts for a critical patient. The flat, shrill tone of the heart monitor indicated her heart had stopped, and it took all his training to stop from breaking down. If the doctor thought he could save Jamila, the man might need Galen's help.

"Computer, hibernation sequence."

"Initialized. Warning. Patient in critical condition. Forty-two point six minutes remaining to reinitialize heart and lung functions before brain death occurs."

The doctor pushed the floating gurney out of the cargo bay. "Galen, keep up. I have to talk to you."

He followed the man, numb with shock. They entered the lift and Torin crowded in after him.

"Okay, we have to act fast. Like I said, my team can save her, but she'll never be accepted by her people again, so unless you plan to keep her here, I don't know what to do. She could go undiscovered for a while, but the government on Larus, as with many core planets, is very strict about their physicals due to diseases and the desire to catch the sort of thing we're about to do to her."

"Save her. I don't give a damn."

Torin rubbed the back of his neck. "Galen—"

His hands curled into fists as he fought not to hit his friend. "I was never going to let her leave anyway, Torin."

"Does she know that? Because I'm pretty sure she'll want to go back eventually. What about her father?"

He growled. He refused to let her die, no matter what the cost. She could hate him if she wanted.

The doctor cleared his throat. "I'm leaving it up to you, Galen. She is your prisoner, after all, and I hope, for her sake, more. Usually I'd want to have the patient's approval, but I'm telling you now I won't get that chance."

"I already told you to do it. Do whatever it takes."

The lift slid smoothly to a stop as the doctor regarded him. "Good."

• • •

Galen paced away from Torin for the thousandth time.

"Oh my God. If you don't stop moving, I'm going to knock you out. You're driving me up the walls."

Galen glared at him. "If it was the woman you loved in there, you would be worried too."

He snorted. "I am worried. I like Jamila. How many women have the balls to taser a cyborg and risk braving open space filled with hostiles to survive? And from the short time I've spent with her, I've enjoyed her company. But unlike you, I'm still calm. Barret is probably the best doctor in this galaxy, and he has cyborg technology and genetics at his command."

Galen collapsed into the chair next to him. "But it's been hours."

"Yeah, well, this isn't simple surgery. On a core planet she'd be dead."

Alec slipped into the small room they were waiting in. The grim set of his mouth and stiff movements immediately set Galen on edge. "What is it?"

Alec tilted his head from side to side, cracking his neck. "Look, I know you're having a personal emergency, but we've got some next level shit happening upstairs."

When he didn't continue Galen jumped to his feet. "Well, let's not pause for dramatic effect, Alec. Spill."

"Government ships are on their way. According to our intelligence they were alerted by a tracking device placed in someone on this vessel."

He shook his head. "That's not possible; everyone is scanned on their way out of the cargo bay."

"Yes, but we don't know every tiny piece of new technology they come up with. Something slipped past us. It might even have been activated later. Everyone is having an in depth, three dimensional scan to try and locate the device."

The door to the operating room hissed open.

"And you'll need to be scanned as soon as possible."

"Sure." Galen faced the doctor without giving Alec a second thought, even though his mind screamed that this was the thing to panic about. But he was too worried about Jamila to focus on that. *When did I choose love over my duty to my people?*

"Well, Doc?"

The man beamed. "She'll make it. She's out of it right now. On the good drugs. But they should wear off within the hour."

Relief swept through Galen and he swayed dangerously. Torin grabbed his shoulder and lowered him into a chair.

• • •

"I replaced your heart with one that is mostly mechanical. I altered your genetics enough to accelerate healing. Of course, there are side effects to even that alteration. Immunity to almost any illness. Perfect eyesight. Possibly some increased mental acuity." Barret sighed. "There really are some genetic alterations the core planets should embrace again."

Jamila massaged her temples. If she were capable of getting headaches anymore, she'd definitely have one. "They won't. What am I supposed to do now?"

Galen squeezed her hand. "What you always would have done. Stay here. You'll be safe here with me."

She glanced down at her lap. She loved Galen, and wanted to stay with him, but she'd always hoped that maybe she could go back to see her father. Eventually he would get the charges against her dropped and she would have had enough freedom to travel back to her home. She would miss him. And there were things she wanted that she'd left behind. Pictures of her mother and her home on Earth. Things that couldn't be replaced. What about her friends? Most had been shallow, and stopped hanging out with her once her partying had stopped and she'd ceased blowing ridiculous amounts of money on them, but a few stuck around, and would worry about her.

Here she had no family. She had one person on the entire ship that didn't hate her guts and want her dead. Well, scratch that. The doctor had saved her life, so he must at least be objective enough to realize she was an asset. Torin hadn't killed her yet either.

Her biggest concern was the cyborg Council. She knew they wanted her dead, and everyone but Galen would support them. She didn't want Galen hurt if he decided to fight against them. What kind of life could she have here? Before, she'd wanted to stay. Now she had no choice.

Galen smiled. "Don't look so worried. It will work out."

Barret nodded. "It will. You're almost one of us. You'd never be accepted back home, so it will soften the blow to some cyborgs when they find out who your father is. We can always keep that as well concealed as possible. Though, your face is splashed all over the newsfeeds."

"Barret," Galen growled.

The older cyborg cleared his throat. "Right. Never mind. I need to scan you both for tracking devices. You're the rare few that haven't been checked."

Chapter Twelve

Jamila and Galen sat in complete silence in the tiny shuttle that was headed back toward her planet, and right into the hands of the government.

She sighed. She knew Galen didn't believe her. She wasn't even sure she could blame him for that. After all, how could a person *not* know about a tracking device in their body, especially since it had been implanted deep in her right buttock? It was so deep and larger than the one in her arm that an injection couldn't have put it there. She tried to remember the last time she'd had a surgery or anything that would have given an opportunity for its placement. Anytime in her drug induced, lost party year would have been perfect. She didn't remember the majority of that year—she'd spent most it passed out.

She'd tried to explain all this to Galen, and promised that she didn't know anything about it, but he hadn't even glanced her way since he'd been given the news that she had a tracking device that they'd missed in their initial scans. He'd somberly told the commander of the ship that he would take her back himself so the rest of the crew wouldn't be at risk. Torin had protested, claiming Galen had more of a shot with some wing men covering his ass, but Galen knew this was the last trip he'd take. He'd told Torin as much. Anyone with him was going to be captured with him.

He'd resigned himself to his fate.

It pissed her off. She'd asked if they could remove the tracking device, but he'd been stubborn about it. He was convinced she knew about it, and wouldn't trust her on his ship or the station.

And so he was taking her back.

It hurt that he didn't trust her. She loved him, and he was willing to give her up. But then, he was protecting a whole civilization of people who would be killed if they were found.

She sniffled, unable to hold back her tears. Now that she didn't have a choice, she'd discovered she didn't want to leave. She wanted to stay with him, and the kids he'd saved for her. She didn't want to go back to a world where she wasn't wanted and where the government was going to murder innocent people. She wanted to be a part of resisting them, and helping these people create a life.

"Galen—"

"Be quiet."

"Can't we talk about this?"

"How many times do we have to have this conversation?"

She rammed her fist into his arm and he glared at her. "Until you fucking listen to me, you stubborn bastard."

"You have nothing to say. You betrayed me. That's all it is. I can't really blame you. You were kidnapped for nefarious purposes. You said you'd do what you could to make sure we wouldn't succeed and you've done it."

"Do you really believe I'm capable of this? I was so happy that you'd saved those people from the Haven district. You know how their deaths devastated me."

"But you didn't know about them when you activated the tracker."

She balled her hands in her hair and swallowed a scream. She cleared her throat. "How the hell does someone activate a tracker in their own ass cheek? Explain how I did this. Because I'm at a loss. How did I reach that particular button?"

He growled. "Don't be obtuse. You could do it remotely."

She sighed and massaged her temples in light circular motions. "Doesn't it make more sense that my father activated it to get me back?"

"You'd still have to know about it. It's deep. It's not like the small, injected one in we deactivated in your arm when you came on board. This one you would have to have knowledge of, or it was done while you were in surgery for something else. According to what I've read on you, you haven't had any surgeries in years. This thing is state of the art. It's recent."

"You're also forgetting that last year is a blur of drunken, drug induced nights partying." This wasn't the first time she'd been deeply ashamed of that, and it likely wouldn't be the last.

He shook his head. "I don't want to hear it. My life is about to end, basically. I get to return you, and turn myself in at the same time, so I don't really want to hear your excuses. You were trying to escape two days ago. Why should I believe you didn't turn on a tracking device somehow when you failed?"

Her blood ran cold. "Why are you turning yourself in? Why can't you release me in a life pod?"

"I could, but they know the last location of the ship. Hopefully if I turn myself in, they'll assume that it was only us out here and not a ship full of people and they won't search too hard for it."

"But they'll torture you for information."

He sighed and raked his hand through his hair. "And by the time they break me, the ship will be somewhere else, the space station will be moved, and all my security and communications codes will be changed."

She glared at him. She couldn't let him be taken. Once the government had all the information they thought they could get out of him, they would execute him. And they would probably still search the area for his people. Worse, maybe they would try brainwashing him again. He had too much knowledge to be captured. Surely he knew that. All of his people were in danger if he was caught. Could they really be in more peril if he wasn't?

Now she had to figure out a way to get him on the way back to his people long before she met up with the government officials.

She jammed her finger onto the release of her harness and threw it off before she rose and stormed to the back of the shuttle.

"What are you doing?" he barked, and she had to resist marching back up front and popping him on the back of the head.

"Pacing so I don't start hitting you."

He sighed but said nothing. She glanced over her shoulder to make sure he wasn't looking, and pushed the button to open the life pod. The one she'd tried to take from the cyborg's big ship had been a larger capacity, luxury escape pod. This one was bare bones. Big enough for two. You could input a course and change it but otherwise it was completely on autopilot.

Jamila glanced at Galen again and seized the syringe of sedative secured at the head of the pod. It was for panic attack emergencies.

Galen cursed and jumped out of his seat as she swung back around. Had he seen her pull out the syringe? He marched to her and she threw her arms around his neck.

"I can't let you sacrifice yourself over this." She curled her fingers into his hair and pulled just to let him feel a small portion of her anger. "It's insane. You don't know if they'll even believe you're alone out here with me. What if they keep searching for your people?"

He pulled back. His eyes still held suspicion but the grim set of his mouth softened. "They will always hunt for my people. I need to throw them off the trail until they're hidden."

"If you don't trust me, why are you telling me this?"

He snorted and glanced away. "I don't know. Damn me but I can't seem to shut my mouth around you."

She ducked her head to capture his gaze again. "So you don't think I turned on a tracking device."

He sighed. "I don't know what I think. I want to believe you, and as soon as I give in to that I'll stop thinking. I can't ignore the facts and what it looks like. If it was only me at stake I would, but I can't risk it with all the lives involved."

If she didn't have a goal, she might have smacked him over the head. She blinked back tears and pulled him down for a kiss to cover her reaction. It was a slow mating of tongues and lips. She ran her hands down and cupped his buttocks.

He broke the kiss. "I should get back to the helm."

She didn't let her frustration show in her face. "Did you put the ship on autopilot?"

"Yes but—"

"Then leave it. This won't take long." She released the seal of his flight suit and peeled it over his broad shoulders. She leaned forward and raked his nipple with her teeth before laving it with her tongue. She placed a long, wet line of kisses down his torso as she dropped to her knees.

He groaned. "We really don't have time for this."

She stared up at him. "We do. Besides, don't you want to make time?" Stubborn bastard.

When she licked hollow at his hip he shifted his weight. "Right, we'll make time."

She smiled against his skin. Okay, maybe not that stubborn. Grasping the sides of his suit, she yanked them down before he could change his mind. His thick cock sprang free and she wrapped her hand around it, a shiver passing down her spine. It was too bad that it wouldn't be sliding into her. She couldn't help but get wet for him in anticipation.

She rolled her tongue against the head before sucking his dick into her mouth.

He moaned and threaded his fingers through her hair. "You're amazing."

Clutching his ass with her unoccupied hand, she dug her nails in enough to make his cock jerk in her mouth as he gasped her name. She ran her tongue against the underside of his shaft and sucked hard enough to concave her cheeks.

His stomach muscles clenched as he tried to control the bucking of his hips. She tightened the grip on the base of his dick so he didn't choke her. He shuddered and his cum spurted against her tongue. She jabbed the sedative into his thigh, trusting the automatic injector to flood his system with it.

She swallowed and released his softening cock.

He swayed on his feet and glared at her. "What did you give me?" She rose and tipped him into the waiting escape pod, shoving his flailing legs in after him. He chuckled weakly. "Right, emergency meds in these things. What are you doing, Jamila? I'm turning myself in. They don't need gift wrapping."

Growling at him, she stepped back. "You know, you're an asshole. I'm shipping your back to your people and good riddance because you piss me off. If you trusted me, we could have talked about this, but no. You left me no choice. Surely it's occurred to you that I'm likely going to face trial for supplying Haven? You said it yourself. I would have believed you if you said you didn't turn on a tracking device, but I guess I love you more."

He bared his teeth. "That's not fair. Almost everyone I've ever known has betrayed me. With you being an aristocrat and with who your father is I can't help the doubt. I'm a spy and a terrorist according to your government. I'm in the business of betrayal."

She lost her ability to breathe from the pain in her heart. He would never have trusted her, even if they hadn't found a tracker on her. He'd all but admitted it. He couldn't handle who her father was. "I really don't have time to debate this with you."

He tried to prop himself up on his elbows but collapsed back in the pod with a long blink. "Don't you dare launch this fucking space coffin! There's another very good reason for me to go with you that I haven't mentioned."

She smiled wistfully. "And here I was hoping your last words to me would be a declaration of love. Guess I'm the silly, foolish child everyone thinks I am. Computer, launch pod one toward the last known location of the cyborg ship."

His shout was cut off with a whoosh as the door slammed shut. She walked to the pilot's seat and dropped into it. She would never see him again. It was just as well. No human could be relied on in his world. She'd never be happy with everyone around her despising her, especially when the man she loved had no faith in her. She'd watched the same thing play out with her parents and it had ended in her mother's suicide.

Tears rolled down her cheeks as she rested her head on the control panel and waited to reach her destination.

Chapter Thirteen

His own people were firing on him. Galen barely managed to avoid the next volley as they tried to take out his engines.

"Galen, turn that fucking ship around. You have to come back. They'll kill you long before you can get to her."

"Sorry, Torin. No can do. I have a plan."

Jamila had been arrested before she even set foot off the transport. Since they'd lost the refugees from Haven, they'd decided they needed to prosecute someone. They planned to execute everyone involved in supplying the residents with anything. Until they'd discovered what the cyborg doctors had done to heal her. Now their spy said the government had other plans for her.

Damn that woman. He should have told her everything. He'd planned to take the fall for any charge they threw at her. But he wasn't sure how she'd react. If she wouldn't let him, she would be in danger, and they'd be right back where they started. But his worst fear was that she wouldn't care that he gave his life for her and she might laugh while he did it. That knowledge would have destroyed him.

How could one man be so fucking stupid? She was being tortured and probably believed no one in the universe cared enough to rescue her. That was his fault. He should have been clear about his feelings.

Torin's long steady stream of cursing went on for a full thirty seconds before he took a deep breath. "You always have a plan, dammit. But whatever you're thinking, it won't work. The government has her."

"And what will they do to her if I don't save her?"

Silence met that question. Everyone knew what they would do. There were two options. Execute her, as the government loved to do, or turn her into one of their operatives. It would be perfect. She'd been inside a cyborg ship. Knew how it operated to an extent. Had made friends with some of the cyborgs. Loved one. It would be easy to put her back in place at a different base if they could find one. But he didn't give a damn about that. There would be a lot of torture before they turned her in to that perfect little spy and killer.

Who knew if his people could deprogram her—if they ever even found her? It didn't always work. Even if they managed, she would never be the same again. She'd be ruined. Broken. Like him. He couldn't take that chance.

"You'll have to blow me out of the fucking sky to stop me, Torin."

"Galen, what if you're captured? I didn't support your plan of giving yourself up in the first place. Think, man. You know classified shit, bad things that could ensure that they find us all. It was close enough when you took her back. She saved you for a reason. She didn't want our people to die. She thought your life was worth hers. You're squandering her gift if you go there and get yourself captured."

Rage tore through his gut. He wasn't worth the sacrifice. He still couldn't understand what she'd been thinking. "She's worth it to me."

Torin's long suffering sigh came over the com. "You could at least take backup. Take five minutes and get the Council's backing."

"They'll never agree. Your list of rational reasons to turn my ass around is a good one. Unfortunately for you, I'm not a rational man right now. The Council can maintain their objectivity in this. I can't and I won't."

"Fine, but you could have at least asked for my help. I like Jamila too, Galen. I think she might be worth it. Stop firing at me, and let me follow you. You'll need help."

Galen hesitated. It could be a trick. Torin could wait for him to land, knock him out, and drag him back off the planet. But…"I thought you were never going back to a core planet? That they'd have to drag you back? That you'd never take a mission on one?"

"You're my friend. I'll do this for you. Whether you want me to or not. If you turn me down I'll follow you out of the range of your weapons."

Galen glared at the com system. "Okay. But don't you dare think of knocking me out and taking me home. I'll murder you when I wake up, and I'm not being the least bit funny."

"You're never funny. You lack a sense of humor. I don't know what Jamila sees in you. Old turd. Let me disable my wing brothers, and we'll keep going together."

He nodded. Right. There were still other fighters on his ass. "Need any help?"

"Nope, they'll never see this one coming. And…done. Let's get the fuck out of here. They're efficient. They'll have their engines fixed real damned fast if they're able. Punch it. I'm behind you."

Galen hit full burn and was plastered against his chair. Even his superior strength didn't keep the force of full burn from squeezing the air from his lungs. The pressure eased as the speed leveled out. He should sleep, but he couldn't bring himself to. Instead, he stood and stretched his legs before beginning to pace in his tiny space. He needed to keep thinking about things. The facility she'd been taken to. The plan. Yeah, the plan wasn't a good one. Torin was right. There was no good way to do this. But he had to try. If he died then so be it.

· · ·

When he stepped off the shuttle he immediately pulled his stun gun. He trusted Torin, and loved him like an annoying little brother, but in this he couldn't be sure of him. Torin would try to protect him and their people at all costs, even if he went against

Galen's orders to do it. It was a matter of personal loyalty and Torin's own calculations of the risks. If one or both were lacking, Torin could easily betray him and not bat an eye. He would see it as doing what he thought was best to save Galen's life or their people.

There was a hiss as the ship's ramp broke open and lowered into the grass of the senator's fancy ass lawn. They'd set down at the far reaches of his estate. It was a big risk to even land here, but the senator was part of the plan. They didn't even know where Jamila was being held. They needed him, and if his security from last time was any indication it would be a joke to get to him. Even if he'd beefed it up, it was still a bunch of humans, content in the knowledge that their guns would do their jobs for them. He snorted. Guns were great, but you still had to know what the fuck you were doing with your tactics. Since he and Torin were stealthy, they wouldn't even be spotted until it was too late. The humans could probably locate their ships and sound the alarm quickly, but finding them? Not as easy.

Torin stepped onto the plank and Galen leveled the stunner on him. He quickly held up his hands to show he was unarmed. Galen wasn't fooled. Torin's hands themselves were weapons. He rivaled Galen in hand to hand combat. And his own guns, stunners, and blades were in their holsters around his hips. But he was making an effort to reassure Galen that he wasn't trying to take him home.

"I told you man. I want to help. She doesn't deserve to be left wherever they're keeping her. You're right. They'll torture her. We both know what that's like."

Torin especially. He was still suffering from what they'd done to him. He'd been a child when they'd taken him. Not even having a life, and then suddenly being deprogrammed and finding out they'd murdered your parents, stolen your childhood, and made you a killing machine had made him unstable for a long time after he'd come around. He was the youngest taken that Galen knew of. At least Galen had known what it was like to have a life. But it was another reason why he was worried about Torin's actions now. He could be unpredictable. He didn't think like the rest of them.

Galen reluctantly holstered his stun gun and Torin lowered his palms slowly.

"There you go. See, I haven't attempted to knock you over the head yet. Satisfied?"

"We'll see."

Torin rolled his eyes. "Good God. You are the most paranoid man I've ever met. I'm your friend and you don't trust me."

"I can barely bring myself to trust anyone. It's an unfortunate cyborg trait."

He snorted. "True enough. Now let's get a fucking move on before someone discovers us here."

The crept through the grounds silently. No one sounded the alarm, even when they entered the house. There were no guards waiting for them. Nothing. It was too quiet. What was going on?

"Galen, this is giving me the creeps. Where are the guards? Where are the servants? Where are the houseguests? Do you think he's taken the household somewhere else?"

Galen groaned. He hadn't thought of that. With his daughter not in residence, he might have closed the SkyTemple. There was no reason to keep it running if no one lived here.

"The senate will meet again soon. He might have left early for that."

Torin cursed. "What now?"

He shrugged. "Let's keep searching the place. We haven't combed over the entire house."

They gave up sneaking around and walked the rest of the house openly. They reached the breakfast nook where Jamila had bought him and he hesitated at the door. Was he ever going to see her again? His doubt gnawed at his gut. Once the government had someone, they chose when to let them go. But he would die trying to find her. He'd have to send Torin packing so the man wouldn't die with him. Damn Torin and his loyalty. He was going to let Galen lead him right into death. He sighed and opened the door.

The senator stood on the balcony with his back to them. "Took you long enough, Galen."

He charged toward the man. Torin shouted his name but that didn't slow him down. He just saw red. He shoved Cyrus against the guardrail hard enough to knock the breath out of him. He lifted him and flung him over the side, grabbing his ankle to keep him from falling to his death.

"Where is she? I won't hesitate to kill you if they've hurt her. Tell me where!"

"Pull me back up." Panic laced the man's voice and Galen smirked.

Torin grabbed his arm. "Are you crazy? If you drop him we'll never find her."

"Believe me, I won't drop him. If he falls it will be because I decided to let go. He's going to talk."

"Pull me up. Please!"

Torin gripped his other flailing leg and tugged. Galen growled at him and Torin shoved him with his other hand. Galen released Cyrus's ankle and Cyrus screamed as he swung from side to side.

Torin grunted, but easily kept a hold of him. He yanked him up and all but threw him onto the floor.

Cyrus scrambled to the pillars of the guardrail and clutched one. "Damned cyborgs. You're all crazy."

Galen flung his arms wide and smiled. "We are what you made us, old man."

Torin gaped at him. "Wow, you've lost it over this chick, haven't you?"

"Shut the fuck up."

He reached for the senator again but Torin knocked his hand away. "I understand your fury, but this isn't the time. My God.

Things have taken a turn for the worst when I'm the sane person." He turned on the senator and crouched next to him. "You're going to tell us where she is."

"Of course I am. I want my baby back. She means everything to me. And I can't get her out without you damned people."

It was then Galen realized Cyrus Clearborne's eyes were red and swollen from crying. Good. He deserved pain. If it hadn't been at Jamila's expense, he would have left the old boy to it.

"So you need our help?"

"Yes, dammit. She'll be too weak to move. She might even fight us if we try to take her. I don't know exactly what's been done to her, but I have an idea."

Galen growled at him. "Of course you do. They're using your methods."

"And I can use them to fix her."

Galen couldn't control his temper and moved to hit him. Torin seized his fist before it made contact. "You'll kill him."

"You can't fix her. You'll never be able to fix her. You put a tracking device in her, and look what's happened."

Cyrus pushed himself to his feet. "This happened because of your lack of medical facilities. I want her back anyway."

"You don't get her back. She's mine! You can't keep her safe anymore."

Their voices rose at the same time.

"She's my daughter."

"You have no right to her anymore."

"Shut up!" Torin shouted above the din of their voices. "We have to figure out how to get her out. We can debate who gets her later, because believe it or not, the woman has a mind of her own and the choice is really hers. Sad, when I respect her more than her father and the man who loves her."

Their glares would have killed a weaker man.

"We need a plan, not a shouting match."

Galen raked a hand through his hair. "A plan."

Cyrus leaned against the wall and crossed his arms over his chest. "Getting in will be the easy part. I have access. But if we're seen carrying her, they'll sound the alarm and we won't make it to the surface."

"Why do you still have access? Still experimenting on people, Doc?"

He stiffened. "I am consulted from time to time on problem cases."

"People that won't automatically bend to the government's will?"

"Yes. Do you want to continue talking about this or do you want to get out of here? It will take us several hours to reach the location where they're holding her."

• • •

The ride to facility was tense, filled with bouts of silence and others of ferocious arguing to the point that Galen worried he would kill the senator. He took another deep breath, and continued counting to ten. He was actually at five hundred forty-seven. So much for that coping technique.

They needed Cyrus. They couldn't get in without him. There were several access points on the way down that needed his key card, security code, and retinal scan. He'd even said something about a DNA check. But if they played the obedient cyborg bodyguards, they wouldn't need to be tested. They would be admitted without being searched for anything but weapons. They'd be permitted one stunner and a knife, for the purposes of defending the senator.

Had they already turned Jamila against them? Would she ever be the same?

The senator cleared his throat. "Don't look so concerned, Galen. I can fix whatever they've done to her. They might use my techniques but they don't know everything I do. Nor do they know Jamila. I'd be very surprised if they'd made any headway in the mere two days she's been there. And as I said, I can fix it."

"You don't get it. You can't fix it. You ruined us. Took our lives away."

"It's not the same. When Jamila comes out of this she will still have her family, unlike most of the subjects in the past."

"Yes, because you started killing our families not long after my generation. It makes me grateful mine left me."

The man leaned forward. "You know your daughter is still alive, don't you? She's in her early twenties now. However, your wife is dead."

A sense of dread filled his gut. "How do you know that?"

"The families that weren't killed were kept track of. I've met the girl. She's remarkable."

His fist clenched. "Why the fuck have you met my kid?"

He shrugged. "The government had an interest in her. Like I said, she's a remarkable woman. Which I suppose isn't surprising, with you as her father. You were chosen for your ability to do math, your problem solving skills, and your strength, along with many other factors."

"So why wasn't she turned into one of us?"

"Believe it or not, the government has stopped manufacturing your kind. You're too dangerous, and too many of you have turned traitor for it to be a good financial decision to continue with you. They're trying to bury cyborgs and genetic engineering for good. Why did you think the Haven district was blown up? It's happening everywhere. And they're killing off cyborgs they don't need. They want to erase you. Like a bad moment in history."

"Oh God," Torin whispered.

"They'll be coming for you next. They think they've sterilized you, but if they've learned anything, it's that life finds a way, especially if it has access to some incredible medical technology.

They believe that someday your people might be a threat to humanity."

No one could promise they wouldn't be. Tensions were high, and too many things had been done for them to leave the core planets alone.

"Thanks for the information. It will keep my people on alert if I make it back to them."

"As for your daughter," Cyrus shrugged. "The government has hired her for other purposes. Instead of turning her into one of you, they educated her. Took her out of the gutter. You should be grateful."

He wasn't grateful. He was furious and terrified. How dare they go near her! He hated this man for knowing the young woman he didn't. Damn him. The term "manufactured" also pissed him off. His kind weren't toys, and if the government had abandoned cyborgs it likely meant they'd gone on to other more dangerous projects, most likely just as life-destroying for the unfortunate.

"Keep your goons away from my kid."

"Too late. She works for them, and she doesn't work for me so I can't fire her."

He growled and clenched his hands. What could he do? He didn't even know what she looked like. Or what her name was. Her mother had changed both their names when they'd moved. He'd tried to find them once he broke the brainwashing but they'd disappeared.

"Are they going to hurt her? I want her name and location."

The senator considered that. "I have no idea if they'll hurt her. They usually leave employees alone, but since she's yours I expect that she's in danger. Especially since she has a knack for sticking her nose where it doesn't belong. Damned journalists. She's changed her name back to Charlise but added the last name Cole. She should be easy enough to find. Her pretty face has been splashed all over the news lately."

He swallowed and it went down like a ball of lead. "She's a journalist?"

"Yes, she's become a sort of PR person for the government. She probably makes things up to cover their misdeeds."

"Why are you telling me all this?"

His eyes narrowed. "Because she's started searching for you. As a leader in the cyborg project, I've been informed and consulted on how to proceed. Apparently she knows who and what her father is. She seems to wonder what happened to the cyborgs, and won't take the fact that we killed most of them for an answer. She seems to think there's more to it. She's right, of course. But if she keeps going forward with her investigation it could get her killed."

His mind raced with possibilities. He had to do something to stop her, or get her away from them. Cyrus was right; digging into his past would get her killed.

Torin glanced at him from the pilot's seat. "Galen, you have to stop her."

He shook his head. "One problem at a time. We need to finish this mission before I start worrying about what my offspring is up to."

The senator nodded. "A good plan. When you decide on something, I'll help implement whatever plan you come up with if it's a good one."

"Why would you help me? You hate us."

"But my daughter loves you. There must be something worth loving. She's a very particular girl. And your daughter is unique as well. I don't want her hurt. She reminds me a lot of my own child."

He took a deep breath and shook his head to clear it. He couldn't think about this now. They'd get killed if he stopped to worry about her. She was safe for now.

The ship set down gently and he unstrapped his harness. He stood as the senator did. Cyrus reached into the compartment above his chair and pulled out two collars.

"Oh, fuck no. We're not wearing those."

"You have to. No cyborg slave would be without one. The guards will immediately know something is wrong if you don't have them on. They're turned on, but most every function is inactive. Check for yourself." He tossed a collar at Torin. "You do still have the ability to control electronics, do you not? You should be able to at least check for the abilities of these. And even if they were fully active, you could disable them."

Yes, eventually they could break a collar, but it would take a minimum of two hours. And by then he could have easily betrayed them. And while parts of the collar were inactive now, that was easy enough to fix. They were taking a big risk wearing them, but the senator was right. If they didn't they'd be discovered at the first checkpoint.

Torin shook his head. "He's telling the truth, it's not active, but..."

Galen nodded. "I know. But what choice do we have?"

Torin paled and his hands shook as he placed the collar around his throat. "I hate you, Galen. We don't need wrist bands?"

"No, these are updated versions. Galen's slaver had an older model. These will work with only the collar."

Galen snapped his in place. A sick feeling filled his gut and he wondered if he'd made the mistake that would get him killed.

But the senator didn't shout to the guards that they should be arrested. The government officials barely even glanced at them. Odd, considering Galen's list of crimes was longer than his arm. They must not study their own most wanted list very damned often. A mistake on their part.

As they passed the first checkpoint, the tension in the senator's shoulders eased. "I was worried they'd recognize one of you. But then again, your files have been buried for so long everyone assumes you're dead."

Torin snorted. "Yeah, but we're stealing ships constantly. Can't believe they wouldn't make our faces known."

The man arched an eyebrow. "Really? We didn't know who was stealing our ships. We assumed it was pirates."

Galen growled. "Torin, you have a big mouth."

He shrugged. "I assumed they knew we were stealing them. So did you."

Torin had a point. Even pirates weren't bold enough to take from the government. They'd have to be crazy. He nodded.

"Time to stop talking now, gentlemen. You're silent watchdogs. Nothing more."

They both straightened to the rigid posture they'd been trained to hold. It was ingrained in them. Something they'd tried hard to forget, but never quite managed. Though, it had been a long time since they'd practiced. Lapsing into chatter and jokes was normal now unless they were in a combat situation.

They continued to pass manned and unmanned checkpoints without a problem. They'd passed so many that Galen thought his head was going to explode. How many could there possibly be? The government hadn't been this paranoid about the project when he was in it. Though, since they'd started escaping, the policies had been changed. Still, this was getting ridiculous.

They stepped out of an elevator and the senator sighed. "That's it." He turned right and started walking briskly down the hall.

"Now, I have a question. Why do they think you're so devoted that you wouldn't rescue your own daughter?"

He glanced over his shoulder but kept moving. "Because I showed no emotion when they took her, only anger and disappointment in her. I'm not proud of it, but it did keep me in the loop. Of course, they still won't tell me what's being done to her, and once she's moved from this facility I'll have no contact. But for now, she's in processing, so I'm still allowed to see her. We have hours before that changes, if we aren't too late."

He stopped in front of a door at the very end of the hallway they'd turned down. "This is it. I'm warning you, keep her restrained until we are well on our way out of here, and remove that tracking device as soon as possible."

He grabbed Galen's hand and slapped a memory chip into it. "This has a code that will allow you to scan for every kind of tracking device the government uses. I suggest you use it on anyone who goes on a mission outside of your facility. And definitely use it on her."

He pressed his thumb to the panel on the door. There was a small beep and it slid open.

She was slumped in a chair in the middle of the room. There was blood on her temples where they'd probably tortured her while trying to brainwash her.

Galen's stomach roiled as he stumbled to her. He collapsed next to her, but didn't dare try to wake her. What if she cried out and tried to get them caught? He silently started undoing the straps that held her to the chair.

Her father crouched down next to him. "Try not to wake her."

"I know," he ground out through clenched teeth. "We have to get her out of here, so we're going to have to move her at some point. Maybe we should gag her."

Cyrus nodded. "Sounds cruel, but it's probably a good idea. I don't know if they sedated her or not. Probably not. She probably passed out."

"Think there's tape anywhere?"

Torin thumped him on the shoulder and Galen glanced at him to find he had a roll. "What the hell are you doing with tape?"

"Remember back when I thought I was going to have to knock your ass out and drag you home? Tape is good and portable for that. Nothing works quite like it. Besides, this stuff isn't supposed to pull off skin. Kidnapper's Tape is what they call it where I'm from."

"Oh, now that's fucked up. And you think that would actually hold me?"

His eyes went blank. "Held me once."

Galen didn't ask. All of them had pain, and secrets from the past, and none of them were cool with sharing it. "Glad you have it."

He snatched it from him and started winding it around Jamila's wrists. He slapped a length of tape over her mouth before throwing her over his shoulder. "Now what?"

Cyrus glared at him. "Now we get out of here."

Torin coughed like he was covering a laugh. "And how the hell do we do that? We passed seven checkpoints to get down here."

Cyrus marched to the door. "There's more than one way out. We have a shorter, emergency exit. We'll have to make it there unseen. Our ship will be waiting."

Great. It was a better option than going back the way they came, but they'd have to get there without being caught. No sure thing.

"Also, as soon as we open the exit silent alarms are going to go off. We'll have two minutes, maximum, to get out of here before ground troops arrive. Five for aerial pursuit."

Galen cursed. "We can't make it off planet that fast. It's not possible."

"We're going to have to. I was hoping you and Torin had some sort of flight skill."

Torin nodded. "I can do it. We'll full burn as soon as we lift off. We won't make it back to the station, but we'll set the beacon off. Our people will be looking for us, and unless the government knows our frequencies they won't be able to pick up the beacon."

Galen glanced at the senator. "Do they?"

"Not that I know. But I'm no longer kept completely in the loop. I'm a consultant, and I never dealt in tactics or intelligence even before."

"Dammit. Hopefully they don't have anything, or we'll be screwed."

Torin shrugged. "We have to chance it. I don't see another way. If we don't go full burn, we'll be caught. Our little jumper is faster but they'll overwhelm us by sheer numbers. It's dangerous if we don't leave quickly. If it comes to the worst, then I do have a friend in a very low place that will get us there. For a price. Michael is a pirate, but he's alright people."

Galen snorted. "A rousing endorsement."

"Well, I could lie, but that won't get us anywhere."

Galen strode to the door, and peeked out. "All clear. Let's move."

They moved silently this time. The senator took each corner alone to make sure no one was there. They would have to duck into a room if someone was coming.

"We're close—one more corridor and we're free." He turned the corner and froze.

"Dr. Boris, it's good to see you."

Fuck. Torin and Galen slipped backwards and Torin pulled on door handles to find an empty room to duck into.

Jamila groaned and shifted on Galen's shoulder and he froze. *Come on, baby. This is not the time to wake up.* Torin waved at him frantically and he dashed for the door the man held open. He silently shut it behind them and leaned against it.

Galen glanced around the room and spotted a cyborg frozen in a chair, gaping at them.

"Shit, Torin, are you nuts? There's someone in here."

"We didn't have a choice. Everything else was locked. I don't know why this dude's cell wasn't."

The man growled low in his throat. "Because this isn't a cell. I'm here by choice."

"Dude, you're strapped to a chair."

His eyes narrowed. "It's to keep me still during the experiments."

Galen felt bile rise in his throat. He'd been there before. They needed to get this man out. But they couldn't risk it. Not when he was well and truly working for them.

"Someday we'll get you out."

The man's upper lip curled into a sneer. "I don't want out. This is where I belong. I'm doing a job I enjoy. The government knows what's best for its citizens. I'm doing good work and you're a traitor. You'll see the light or you'll be executed. I hope I'm there for that."

Torin glared at him. "Can we shut him up?"

Galen shook his head. "Nope. I remember giving those speeches to the men who rescued me. He'll spout the government's good intentions until he loses his voice. What do you think drove my wife away? She said I scared her, but I'm convinced my political speeches made her stark raving mad."

Torin chuckled but it was hollow. "We can't get him out, can we?"

Galen sighed. "No, but at least we know about this place. We'll send a team in to liberate it." His hands trembled with rage. "I hate this shit. They need to leave people alone. Get real recruits for their armies. Something. Anything."

The new cyborg shouted. "There are traitors in here. Traitors. Somebody stop them. They're taking a woman."

Jamila jerked on his shoulder and tried to sit up. He shifted her on his shoulder so she fell back down his back. She screamed under the tape and hit his ass with her bound hands.

"Easy, girl. Come on. It's Galen, stop screaming. Sit tight and we'll get out of here."

She didn't pause in her screaming and his heart sank. She was brainwashed. She might not even remember who he was, and even if she did, she'd never believe he was here to help her.

Torin stepped behind him. "Hey, Jamila, come on. Snap out of it. We're here to help you."

Her struggles and screaming suddenly ceased. Her hands balled in the back of his shirt and instead of hitting him, a muffled noise that sounded like it could be his name came from her.

He ran his hand up the back of her thigh. "Relax. We're getting you out of here. We have to keep you tied. We don't know if you're—"

His voice broke and he couldn't finish his sentence. But she didn't try to pound his back again, and the screaming ceased.

The senator poked his head in and the cyborg started shouting again. They quickly rushed out of the room and shut the doors.

"Let's get out of here. Now. Everyone on this planet probably heard that bastard shouting."

The whoop of an alarm made everyone jump.

"Fuck. Run."

They made a mad dash for the door at the end of the hall, following the senator's lead.

He pressed his thumb to the exit's key panel and there was a loud buzz. The light above the door flashed red and it didn't open.

"Shit. The facility is in lockdown."

Galen glanced at Torin. "Try to kick it down, while I go in through the computer system."

Torin immediately lifted his foot and pounded it against the door. Galen closed his eyes and started hacking the system. Their safe guards were up. He had to watch his back. Once they'd determined that cyborgs could hack their computer systems, they'd started adding special viruses when safety systems went off. Viruses that could kill a cyborg by shutting down the computer that controlled his brain. Boom, dead. It wasn't a way Galen wanted to go. And that was if they wanted you dead. He'd seen one man hacked and go right back to the government. All the deprogramming wasted. Galen was the superior hacker, which was why he'd asked Torin to take on the door.

He found the switch for the door and tripped the locks. It burst off its hinges as Torin kicked it one last time.

They rushed onto the ground and ran headlong for the waiting shuttle. The wiz of stun guns being discharged filled the air. Jamila curled tighter onto his back, and screamed. Torin dropped like a stone in front of him.

Chapter Fourteen

Galen snatched Torin's hand and dragged him the rest of the way to the ship, and up the ramp. His foot caught the edge and he fell the rest of the way, yanking Torin with him. Jamila squeaked as he came down hard on her legs. She managed to stay sitting and not whack her head on the floor. Cyrus sank into the pilot's seat.

Galen took a deep breath and shouted. "Computer, close the doors and lift off. Now. Don't wait for the doors to close fully."

"Unadvisable."

"Do it, you piece of shit."

"Affirmative."

"Damned straight."

Bitingly cold air whirled around them as the ship shoved itself at full speed into the air. The gears closing the door screamed in protest, but kept moving. The ramp slammed closed and he breathed a sigh of relief.

"Computer, full burn. Head for the following coordinates." He kept the coordinates to himself as he transmitted them directly to the ship.

He gripped Jamila and Torin tight as they jolted forward.

When the pressure lifted the senator sighed and turned in his chair. "That was close."

"Don't jinx us. We aren't out of danger yet. If we get into trouble we're screwed. Torin is the superior pilot, and he's out."

They waited in silence for the telltale rocking of the ship that would signal they were being fired upon. Nothing happened.

He sat up, carefully taking his weight of Jamila's legs.

159

She slowly pulled the tape off her mouth. "Why the hell am I taped? Let me out."

Torin groaned and sat up clutching his head. "I hate those fucking stunners. I'm going to have a migraine for days."

"Yes, how terrible for you. At least you're not tied up. Galen, come on, loosen my hands."

Torin grinned. "Nope, you get to stay like that until we're back on a bigger ship, and one of our doctors can check you out."

Her gaze snapped to his. "Galen?"

"Yep. That's the deal. We don't know if you've been brainwashed or not."

She glanced away. "They tried. They—"

He grabbed her and pulled her into his lap, wrapping his arms around her. "You don't have to talk about it now. We'll talk about it later. In private." He wasn't sure he could hear what they'd done to her now. Not without turning their jumper around and going on a suicide mission to do as much damage as possible. Besides, he was sure she would regret telling those things in the company of Torin and her father. Not that they would mock her, or be bad listeners, but it was a very private matter.

Her eyes welled with tears and she nodded before laying her head against his chest. He had to resist the urge to squeeze her against him.

"I should have been straight with you that day in the shuttle. I had more than one reason to come back with you. I was going to take the fall for you. I suspected you would be wanted for supplying the Haven district. I love you, and I couldn't let them execute you for that."

She pulled back and looked up at him and he wiped tears off her cheek with his thumb. "What did you say to me? Something about love?"

He smiled and pressed his lips against her forehead. "I love you, Jamila."

"It's about damned time you said it."

He snorted. "I've loved you since I found out you were giving food and medical supplies to people in need, even when the government said it was wrong."

Her father cleared his throat sharply. "I don't like this. I cooperated with Galen to save you, not so you could run off and marry him. I don't want you associating with them. They're dangerous criminals."

Rage boiled in the pit of Galen's stomach. He'd kill this man before he let him take back his daughter. "We are what you made us. We're tired of doing horrible things to help subjugate others. Besides, you have no choice. She's wanted now. And most importantly she's mine. I won't give her up because you have a problem with my people."

Her father crossed his arms over his chest. "Maybe I won't help you find your daughter if you don't?"

Torin snorted. "How about we hold you captive and torture you until you do."

Jamila pressed her fingers over her ears and squeezed her eyes shut.

Cyrus rolled his eyes. "That won't work. Where the government wasn't willing to commit its full resources to finding my daughter, it will come after you if you take me. I know too many secrets, and too many men are counting on me to vote their way on several issues. Several issues you would find very important, that I could help you with." He leaned forward, placing his elbows on his knees and lacing his fingers together. "You think life is hard now? What if the government unleashes its full wrath on you? You might think they've been hunting for you, but they haven't even been trying. And if you don't do exactly as I ask, things could get very bad for you."

Jamila threw her bound hands up in there air. "Shut up! Really, you're going to discuss this now? You can't wait to threaten the man I love and try to take him away from me? I know you want your world to be exactly like you want it, but doesn't my happiness mean anything to you?"

Cyrus straightened, grimacing in pain. "I want what's best for you."

"And that's Galen. Even being captive on his ship I've felt more alive than I have in the past year. Maybe longer. Doesn't that matter?"

The old man's eyes glistened with tears and he glanced away. Galen never suspected that the bastard had a heart, but he clearly felt something.

"I love you, Jamila. I don't think I can live without you. I'm already living without your mother. It was my fault that she killed herself. She felt ridiculed, and unloved, and let it consume her. I want to keep you close. To protect you."

"And by taking Galen from me, you'll be making the same mistake twice. I'm wanted in the core planets now, as well as ridiculed."

"I can find a safe place where you'll survive."

"I don't want to survive. I want to *live*. I want freedom, and love, and most importantly I want to help those people on that ship. People that are injured. People that lost everything because the government you work for thinks they deserve to die. You're going to help Galen find his daughter, and you're going to vote favoring the genetically engineered and the cyborgs from now on. Please, Daddy."

He nodded. "I don't know if I can bear not seeing you again."

She stood and stumbled to his side. She clasped one of his hands in hers. "If you can fix this war with the cyborgs, maybe someday you will."

"You come back to me if you're ever unhappy."

Annoyance flared but Galen kept his trap shut. This was their moment. But he would make sure she was always happy from now on.

Cyrus cleared his throat. "Torin, get up here and set this thing down on the third planet."

"Daddy, what about helping me escape? What will they do to you?"

He snorted. "Don't worry about that. I'll lie and say I was coerced. No one will believe me and I'll get death threats. Thus is the life of a politician. I'm hoping I won't get assassinated helping these people."

He patted her hand when panic flashed across Jamila's face. "I'm joking, pumpkin."

Everyone knew that was a lie, but she didn't press him about it.

•••

Jamila leaned on Galen as they walked back from the infirmary. She'd been thoroughly checked for every device they could conceive of. She'd also had some annoying little gnat of a psychiatrist analyzing her for brainwashing and secret orders, and whatever other worries they had. When they determined she had no weapons, no tracking or communication devices, and was not going to snap and kill someone, they'd released her. Though she'd been told she was still required to meet with the psychiatrist weekly, and she would be watched. It was creepy, but they had good reasons.

"I'm so tired, Galen. I don't think I've slept since I was taken into custody."

He squeezed her shoulder. "We're almost there."

He'd been tense and silent since her father had disembarked from their shuttle. She could tell he was worried about her.

She glanced at him. "Galen, I can't talk about it. They didn't have long, but they were...inventive."

She flinched as horrific images of the violence and death they'd showed her flashed through her mind. The remembered pain echoed through her limbs.

She jumped when Galen pressed a finger over her lips. "Don't think about it. Don't worry about telling me. I remember. And one day, when you can talk about it, you'll come to me, and I'll always listen. You can tell me anything. And if you feel like you can't, you are required to see that psychiatrist. Tell her."

She nodded as they stepped into Galen's chamber. "I want to forget for a while."

He nibbled her neck. "I can think of an excellent way to forget about it."

She giggled. "Really? Now? What happened to me getting some sleep?"

"Well, we can make time for it. Can't we always make time for this?" He slid his hands into her pants and cupped her mons.

She snorted. "At that time, I was trying to distract you and get you to do what I wanted."

"Well, I want to get laid. We're on the same wavelength here."

She turned in his arms and glared at him, but could quite manage it over the tenuous smile breaking across her face.

"You're lucky you're hot."

He scooped her up and tossed her over her shoulder. "I'll take that as a 'Yes, please do me.' You won't be disappointed."

"I never am."

About the Author

Honoria Ravena lives in north Texas. With a cat for a pet who insists on helping her type her stories, she enjoys yoga, belly dancing, a growing addiction to cosmetics, and reading many types of fiction. You may find her on Facebook and Twitter, but do not be surprised if her cat answers you instead, as Honoria never sits still long enough to be found. Visit her at *www.honoriaravena.com*.

A Sneak Peek from Crimson Romance
(From *Fusion* by Candace Sams)

Reisen Four
Behind enemy lines
Earth year 5037

To save what ammo she had, Lyra Markham jammed the butt of her photon rifle into the face of the charging Condorian. The resulting thud was exceedingly gratifying.

Her foe fell into an awkward heap. His head lolled to one side and his eyes immediately assumed a deathly, hollowed glaze.

It'd been a very good hit.

She tossed her empty rifle aside. It was added weight she couldn't afford.

A quick search of her dead foe's arsenal proved pointless. Though the fool was out of ammunition he'd still had the balls to charge, brandishing a horrific looking, ten-inch boot blade. Aside from that weapon, which she summarily shoved into the barrel of her tall desert boot, there was nothing else to be scavenged from his body. No ammo. No grenades. Nothing.

Scrambling sounds made her glance backward.

Unfortunately her dead enemy's nasty-looking friends witnessed her attack from about a hundred yards away. They grouped for the chase.

As they ran toward her, firing, she ducked and took off northward, as fast as her body armor allowed. She now counted seven Condorians breathing down her neck.

Sweat poured down her face as she gazed ahead, hoping to get to the far, rocky hills where she'd have the advantage of being on higher ground.

As Lyra ran, she was forced to jump over the bodies of Delloids, Capricans, Startsur warriors, and Freermen. All of them were Earth allies in the war against the Condorians. All were spilling blood just as freely.

No matter how many allies came to the front, intending to beat back the enemy ravaging the entire galaxy, the Condorians kept bringing more. The only thing that kept her world and other allied planets from being overrun were these desperate stands in space—diversions meant to slow the enemy while allied commanders fell back and reassessed battle strategy.

Annihilation was only a matter of time. She knew it; so had all the dead lying around her. But no one was giving up. The Condorians wouldn't take hostages. Innocent inhabitants from hundreds of allied planets would die horrible deaths. It now came down to a matter of how one died. Her course was in battle.

She rounded an outcrop of rock and stopped to lean against it, dragging air into her lungs while she could. Every detail of this stinking, blood-soaked battleground blended together.

There were almost no colors on Reisen Four. Sepia-tones obscured some of the rocky escarpments in shadow. There was no grass, sparse plant life of a higher order, and precious little water. Whatever the cost, Lyra vowed not to be taken alive.

Approaching boot steps signaled her brief respite was over. She gripped her sidearm and ran again. She'd have taken her helmet off for better maneuverability, but the only long-range transmitter she had was built inside. Even though she was sure her superiors had given her up for dead, she couldn't relinquish the last communication device available. And some part of the helmet might deflect incoming fire.

As one of thousands of Class M planets, Reisen Four's air was breathable. Lyra and other allied fighters had been given orders to leave air packs behind. In this environment, the oxygen canisters would have weighed fighters down. That brilliant foresight helped her make good time now. But without filtered oxygen, the dirt in the air penetrated every part of her uniform, including the damned helmet. Still, she clung to the last hope that a signal might come from an allied vessel. With her own fighters scattered to the four winds, Earth Forces deployed in this battle were quite gone or dead.

There'd originally been three other women in her platoon. She was the last and had seen the remains of her friends and what had been done to them. That image was burned into her brain and was the only thing keeping her from turning around and shooting into the pack chasing her. Her pursuers had picked up the pace. She was pretty damned sure they knew she was female.

Hours went by. She dodged, hid, and ran but it made no difference. After only a few precious moments to rest in every few hundred yards of running, her foes kept up the pursuit. Their persistence had less to do with losing their friend to her rifle butt, and more to do with catching a woman and slaking their lusts before slowly slaughtering her.

It was now late into what passed for a Reisen Four night. The sepia-tones were only a little darker to delineate the passage of time. She had no idea where she was and didn't care. The Condorians were still running her to ground like hounds on a blood trail.

With her body and wits taxed, she turned into a small, narrowing canyon. Without energy reserves, she suddenly realized she couldn't climb up its side fast enough to keep from being hauled back down the rocky slope. It was there she turned to make what she assumed would be her last stand.

I'll take a few of you bastards with me.

She squared her shoulders, determined to save one last round for her head. She'd be dead before they actually began tearing her apart.

As she raised her sidearm fear gripped her soul. It was then she realized she really wasn't ready to die. A noise from behind signaled she wasn't alone.

In an instant someone from behind clamped a large, strong hand on her shoulder. She was hauled off her feet and bodily thrown into a dark, cavernous space. Her weapon fell from her grasp and she scrambled to retrieve it.

Her attacker pulled her backward. That was the last thing she remembered.

•••

It might have been hours or minutes later when she opened her eyes. She felt her neck being massaged by huge, gentle hands. When her foggy wits cleared, she eventually pushed herself away from the enormous, crouching figure next to her. Since she'd be dead if he was a Condorian; the reasonable assumption was that this darkly uniformed fighter was an ally. He'd most likely saved her life.

"Wh-what the hell happened?" she murmured through her helmet mouthpiece.

Her helmeted savior stared at her.

The huge megalithic creature before her tilted his black, armored head, as if he hadn't heard her correctly. She repeated her question and added more.

"I'm Lyra Markham…Master Sergeant, Tenth Earth Regiment. Who are you and what happened?" she demanded again.

When he kept staring down at her—his face as invisible as hers behind the anti-glare plexi-shielding—she kept trying. "Is your communicator working?" She tapped her head to indicate a communication device that should be located within his helmet.

Since learning that other races occupied the outer reaches of space many centuries ago, universal communication technology had been developed for the benefit of all who wished to speak freely. Unfortunately, better communication hadn't worked with the Condorians. They had but one desire—to take everything and kill anyone who wasn't one of them.

Lyra's comrade continued to stare at her without making a single sound. "Can…you…understand…me?" she asked one last time, enunciating every word quite clearly.

He finally stood and backed away.

From where she sat, she felt at a decided disadvantage. The figure towering over her had to be nearly seven feet tall, as wide as a hatch on a cargo frigate. His shoulders, even without the black, unmarked armor, spanned the distance of a full yard and then some. Unlike her headgear, *his* had a pronounced front-piece that appeared very avian in nature. It was as if the designer was trying to emulate the head of a very large predatory flying creature. She'd never seen its like before. Still, there was no doubt in her mind that he was an ally.

Finally, she hauled her tired frame to a standing position then removed her helmet so he could see her more clearly.

Sometimes these alien beings didn't take to speaking without eye-to-eye contact. She couldn't afford to piss this mountainous person off. He represented the only help available.

Her companion simply tilted his head the other direction and kept staring down at her. She knew she wasn't the most attractive human at the moment. Grime and sweat ran in rivulets over her face, neck, and body. She could feel it even if she couldn't see it. Without oxygen canisters, the body armor was left unsealed so the user could breathe. That resulted in every bit of dirt getting in.

He seemed to study her uniform markings carefully. Even from a great distance, anyone as familiar with allied patches could tell she was an Earther and was ranked Master Sergeant. She'd only announced that fact along with her name and unit designation as a matter of habit. Still, the painted emblem of Earth, surrounded by its telltale starry circle, was clearly emblazoned on her right shoulder and over the left breastplate of her armor. Her helmet had the same emblem plastered all over both sides. He couldn't mistake her origin, but he just wasn't communicating.

She stood for a long moment considering what to do. Her last thought before blacking out had been of death. Not rescue. And this silent giant wasn't helping her overtired brain make sense of the situation.

• • •

Soldar Nar had heard of Earth women being sent to fight on behalf of their world. But her sudden appearance in this desolate, lonely place was utterly astonishing.

Women from his home world of Craetoria simply didn't battle.

Indeed, women in most of the Allied Forces were rare. *This* one was not only in the middle of a very deadly confrontation, but happened to be quite arresting despite the dust and sweat all over her face. Once her helmet was off, he took full stock of a suddenly beguiling sight, something surreal and incomprehensible in this horrible combat zone. Her eyes stared up at him questioningly. Because of the hazy, dirty atmosphere he guessed they might be bright blue. For a moment, he found his mind consumed with the hue. Then he mentally shook himself and considered the rest of her appearance. She didn't seem harmed by his having jerked her into the cave.

Her short brown hair curled just beneath her chin and fell over her forehead in long, wavy wisps. She had a straight, perfect nose that spoke of fine breeding. Her cheekbones were high and elegant. Moreover, her full lips were slightly parted, as if she was about to speak again. Clearly she was as at a loss as he.

Right before he'd grabbed her, the woman had turned to fight her last. Her steadfast inclination to accept fate was apparent in the way she'd leveled her weapon against the oncoming enemy. She'd spread her legs and assumed a stance of absolute resolve.

The exhibition of courage cemented his determination to save this noble ally. At that time, however, he hadn't known this valiant fighter was a woman. He'd believed *her* to be a *he* of very small stature. Now he knew her gender, everything changed.

He felt parts of his body respond magnificently. Except for the absence of a left cheek mark, she could be any woman on his world.

More to the point, he had hadn't seen a woman of *any* race in more than a year. If the Condorians had gotten their hands on this one, he couldn't imagine what she'd have suffered.

Thoughts of his sisters, his mother, and other kinswomen came to mind. If anyone had touched them the way the Condorians would have ravaged this stunning creature, he'd have butchered every last one of them no matter how long it took.

How could Earthers allow their most prized citizens into the middle of battle? Were they really as foolish as others claimed?

He'd seen their men as gallant fighters. Why would they so risk their women? Why would this questioning beauty be in this Creator-forsaken wilderness, fighting all alone and with no hope for survival?

"It's clear there's something wrong with your communicator," she told him. "There are no markings on your uniform but I know damned well you're no Condorian." She suddenly coughed to get a thick layer of dust out of her throat and mouth. When she recovered, she tried to communicate her intentions. "Look…I'm checkin' outta here. You can try to get back to your unit or you can follow me. That second option is best since two of us are more likely to survive." She raised one gloved hand and pointed toward the cave entrance. "We…can't…stay…here. It isn't safe. Those Condorians might be back and the sniveling cowards will come with company. Do you understand?"

He remained silent. His mind just wasn't absorbing her presence. Something deep in his head told him she wasn't supposed to be there. He kept searching for an answer to her presence but his intuition revealed nothing.

"Leave or stay...what's it gonna be?"

He mentally shook himself back into reality and finally responded.

"The Condorians are all dead," he electronically blurted in perfect English. "They didn't call for backup or reinforcements would have been here by now." His helmet speaker blocked more of his voice than hers had. His mouthpiece made his response sound quite automated.

It was her turn to be taken aback. He saw her brows rise. Her pretty, bow-shaped lips fell open, probably shocked to hear him speak her language so proficiently. He was still struck by the twisted situation. Her presence was wrong. He couldn't dispel the shock of it.

Finally, he haltingly raised his hands and considered removing his helmet. This Earther might have never seen a Craetorian's face. His people were ordered to keep their helmets on and speak as little as possible to allied brethren. It was thought that fraternization might prove demoralizing. His superiors believed it was hard enough watching those from one's home world die. How much more difficult would it be to have troops inflicted with the site of newly befriended, slaughtered allies. All this considered, the circumstances surrounding his presence—and hers—called for creativity. His mission came first. He must do what he must. She wouldn't find his face shocking. His features would be the same as her human countenance with but a singular difference.

• • •

Lyra couldn't place his armor or helmet at all but that really wasn't unusual. With so many different worlds fighting the Condorians—whose silver and metallic armor was arrogantly meant to be visible—it didn't matter where any allied warrior originated. All that mattered was that they kept fighting.

There were a few planets, including Earth, whose dignitaries and generals regularly conferred as to battle plans. At Lyra's low rank she wasn't privy to their strategies. She just took orders. So if there was a new, friendly race in the battle she welcomed their presence. It wasn't as if the enemy was running out of fighters.

When her comrade took off his helmet, Lyra barely saw his face in the half light. He seemed to realize his body was shadowed and quickly stepped into a brighter area. This was how she got her first good look at a race that was at the front of every battle. She'd heard of them but had always been sent to fight in areas they weren't present.

"I'm Colonel Soldar Nar, Fifth Planetary Pulsar Unit for Craetoria. At least, my rank translates to Colonel in your language," he announced.

She shook her head in vague recollection. Earth English was rumored to be one of several dialects spoken on his world. Since it was the most universally broadcast, a lot of other races used it. His unexpected familiar greeting made her feel easier. It was a relief to know that neither of them would need any translation devices.

"I've heard of your race," she congenially acknowledged, "but I'm afraid I've never seen one of your people, sir." With that being said, she'd still have recognized the piercing eyes and long blond hair that spilled onto his shoulders when his helmet was removed. The black slash mark originating from the corner of his left eye down his strong cheekbone bore further proof of his heritage. That feature was one of the Craetorian attributes about which her Earth colleagues regularly gossiped. As they'd described, it *did* look exactly like a black electric bolt.

"Where is the rest of your platoon?" Soldar asked.

She briefly lowered her gaze.

"I see." He gestured to the empty cave around him. "My insertion team met the same fate when we landed. I heard the howling of those brutes chasing you and knew some allied fighter was their target. I took position in this cave and waited, but you'd turned to fight off the whole pack by yourself." He waited for her response, but she made none. "I apologize for having incapacitated you, but it was necessary. As I said, I don't believe they had time to call for backup or we'd have been attacked." He sighed, pushed his hair away from his face, and turned his head away to spit dust out of his mouth. When he gazed on her again, his words conveyed his admiration. "You're quite the bold one, Sergeant. The cowards had you at seven-to-one."

Lyra snorted. "Sir, couldn't you have just called out that you were here? Then we could have taken that pack together."

"I hadn't time. And I'm not supposed to be seen by anyone, not even one of the allies. I've told you, I was part of an insertion team. I'm under top secret orders. That means *you're* under those orders now."

"Excuse me?"

"I'm pulling rank, Sergeant. General Elias Shafter sent us here. I'm in his command. That makes me, as ranking officer, your superior. And no, you may not ask why an Earth general is issuing orders to a Craetorian colonel."

"Christ! I don't even want to guess," she readily confirmed as she straightened her body armor and shook her head in amazement. "Whatever the hell is goin' on...I don't mind you being responsible. I'm just here to fight." She shrugged and stared up at him. "So what're our orders?"

"I suggest you get some rest. We sit tight for another hour. Then we move due east."

She watched him lean against a far wall and toss back the thick blond hair that, even in the dim light, draped down his body like a shimmering cloak. She surmised his helmet would be back in place before they left the cave, otherwise that glowing pelt would be plainly visible in the half light of the Reisen Four evening. The presence of such long hair was another unusual characteristic of his race. Locker-room gossip had bestowed some very godlike characteristics on his people.

Was it true they were stronger than almost any other ally and could fight like madmen? Could they go without water for days, and did they have no problem eating rodents and insects they found under logs and rocks?

She tried not to smile as she recalled other, more intimate gossip concerning his race.

Was it true they made love with all the stamina of a photon infusion engine? Were they able to please their partners so thoroughly that their mates stayed by their sides for life?

She looked away before he caught her staring, but lifted one hand to her own short locks. They were matted and dirty. She was sure they didn't shine the way his thick mane did.

When she'd first left Earth as a cadet, she'd had her entire head completely shorn. Over the years, she'd let it grow and now kept it below ear length. It fit uniform codes, was easy to maintain, and didn't obstruct her view. Nobody out here cared what she looked like. Even the Condorians didn't give a damn. That she was a woman was enough for them.

For some odd reason, she wondered about the women of *his* world. Was it true they were as tall as the men? Did they crave Earth chocolate so much that they'd really smuggled it through blockades?

She shook her head. The inappropriate nature of these queries was obvious. What did any of that matter? None of them would live long since the Condorians couldn't be stopped. There were so damned many of them. They'd taken over almost half the galaxy and were on their way to finish the job.

As she leaned against a wall and slid to the ground, she looped her hand on her now empty holster. The hole where her weapon *should* be made her go rigid. She gazed down at it and felt her heart begin to pound.

"Son-of-a-bitch! I lost my sidearm. It's still out there somewhere." She stood and quickly began to search the immediate area around her before making her way outside the small cave.

"You didn't lose it," he advised as he pulled her weapon from under his armor. "I picked it up after rendering you unconscious. I only had three volleys and hoped you had more. Luckily you did."

"Sir?"

"I took out seven Condorians so we now have two volleys left. Both of them are in my weapon. The men chasing you had no remaining laser power. It appears they intended to do you in with one of these."

He showed her a long knife within his right boot top, then carefully handed back her empty sidearm.

She angrily slid her empty pistol back into its holster. The top of the Condorian blade she'd liberated still stuck out of her own boot. "I know you must have been firing fast, sir, but couldn't you have left me one round…in case I get caught?"

"Master Sergeants who lose their weapons don't deserve spare rounds."

She scowled. "Sir, you clearly saw my uniform. You could have stood beside me and helped. Instead of acting like any other ally, you rendered me unconscious, emptied the only weapon I had, and are now insinuating I was careless in losing my sidearm. I hardly think that's a fair summation—"

"Cool off, Earther. It was a joke."

"By the way…what *did* you do to me?" she asked as she rubbed the back of her neck.

"I used a lateral vascular neck restraint. I think that's the politically correct term nowadays for a choke hold." He smiled. "Its effects are only wearing off, or you'd have been questioning me about my actions sooner."

She put her hands on her hips and glared at him.

"I am sorry about taking you to the ground," he apologized. "But when I grabbed you, you turned to fight. I had a few seconds before that pack came barreling down the canyon. I didn't have time to answer questions."

"I suppose this is the part where I'm supposed to thank you?"

"Your sarcasm isn't welcome, Sergeant. I should have left you safely in this cave, coming back to consciousness on your own, without seeing me." He shrugged. "I had a surge of conscience and couldn't leave a comrade alone in this wasteland. You've seen me now and I've conscripted you for a mission. My actions make me responsible for your safety."

"Really? I thought that was *my* job."

"Get over it," he shot back. "We're a team now, whether either of us likes it or not. But to set the record straight as to your ability to look after yourself, I require an answer to just one question."

"Sir?"

"Why did you run into a canyon with no outlet? Were you not properly briefed about how many were present in this area? You're a supervisor. Did you not check maps before landing to fight?"

She rolled her eyes and let out a long, frustrated sigh. "Okay…I made a wrong turn. I screwed up!"

"I can live with the explanation, though you may *not* have. Let's just say we've both had better days. You and I have survived to learn lessons."

"What lessons?"

"You won't run into dead-ends…and I won't lose my weapons, inclusive of all the ammunition, or my entire team!"

He stood, angrily thrust his helmet back on his head, and stalked toward the cave entrance. Once there, she saw him gaze outside.

She finally understood.

He was feeling guilt over surviving. When she'd run toward him—being chased by Condorians bent on peeling her skin off—he saw his chance at vengeance. She'd just been in his way.

This cave, wherever it was, was probably the place where he and his team were supposed to have waited until later in the night. Then, they'd probably have gone about finishing whatever mission they'd planned. But, like so many plans the allies composed, nobody could maneuver against twenty-to-one odds. As she saw it, they were both lucky to be alive.

She almost let the incident go. However, her rescuer now had two shots in his weapon. He'd used hers on the enemy and that situation had to be addressed. She pulled on her helmet and approached him once more.

"Sir?"

"What now, Sergeant?"

"If we get caught you've got all our firepower. Will you make sure they don't take me alive?"

He turned his helmeted head toward her. "Count on it, Sergeant Lyra Markham!"

The corners of her mouth lifted.

His powerfully worded promise to see her die painlessly was acceptable. They now had the makings of a team. For however long they lasted.

In the mood for more Crimson Romance?
Check out *A Demon in Waiting*
by Holley Trent
at *CrimsonRomance.com*.

Printed in the United States
By Bookmasters